Abbey K Davies

I0549936

Finding Home

Abbey K Davies

Abbey K Davies

Published by: Kristen L. Baker

ISBN: 978-0977035069
ISBN-13: 0977035069

DEDICATION

I dedicate this book to the children who have been abused in any manner. To all the heroes that have lived with the secret and lived life to the fullest and never gave up. I dedicate this book to two foster kids that I had the privilege of meeting and knowing they too have found their homes.

To all who have been victimized by alcoholics or addicts. To the child that grew up not finding home. To anyone who has been the victim of abuse of any kind.

Always remain true to yourself and never forget the key: it was not your fault.

DISCLAIMER

This book is for a mature audience. There is sexual abuse, rape, domestic violence and detailed sexual activity. Some words are profane.

I do not mean to insult or bring up bad memories for any reader. I apologize in advance for any offense. It was my intent to have t he reader come away after reading that life can go on and happiness can be had.

This book is for 18+

This is a fictional story.

Finding Home

Abbey K Davies

ACKNOWLEDGMENTS

I would like to acknowledge my husband, primarily for believing in every story I write and for giving me the confidence to share my voice.

Thank you for the beta readers who took time out of their own lives to read this work. Barb, Liz, Heather, Mindy, Teresa, Kim, Myra, Leigh Ann, Alyssa, Pam, Laurna, Rebecca, Susan, Sophia, Amy, Philomena. Lina and Sue.

Thank you to the bloggers that have helped me get the word out about this book.

Thank you to the readers and your dedication to follow my writing.

Thank to my parents for always giving me a home filled with love.

Abbey K Davies

Its quarter after nine and I still can't get my lazy ass out of bed because I'm fantasizing about him. His eyes, the crispness of that color, like a common peafowl peacock with a tantalizing, shadowy blue-green shine to them. His hair, so thick and ready to have my hands linger through it. His legs, a sprawling 6 foot 2 and that jaw, tight and strong, simply gorgeous and out of my league.

How will I ever be able to start my day with these visions swirling around in my head? He doesn't even know I exist. Even if he did, would he then know I exist? There's nothing special about me, I'm a measly 5 foot 5 inches, normal, no big boobs or anything that stands out, except for the scars, of course. I'm just me, the average girl from New Hampshire. Felicia Westfield, twenty-six year- old, never been married but have had a string of bad relationships, romantically and otherwise and lots of therapy. I've lost so much of myself along the way, my heart and my entire being.

Always doing the right thing it seems and it hasn't gotten me anywhere. The do-gooder if you will, never really let my hair down. I would like to let my hair down with him, Jake Brown. I would like to whip my ponytail across the room and slap my hair over his chest as I suckle on his nipples. Just the thought of him brings about sensations and urges I've never had before. A girl can dream. I must get up. Hot Yoga is calling me; perhaps some of this tension will be sweat out of me.

As I get up and go into the bathroom, I look in the mirror and I really look at who is looking back at me. My brown highlighted hair is like Jennifer Aniston's. My eyes are brown and glow of loneliness and pure sadness. My teeth are straight and when I smile at myself in the mirror, I see actual beauty in this moment. I suddenly feel alive. I never felt pretty or stunning but at this moment, I think I look pretty. In this moment, I feel like I could get noticed.

Excitement began rushing through my veins. I just have to see him again. I smile to myself and I realize that I'm much prettier when I smile. Smiling hasn't come easy for me in the past 3 years. In this moment, the smile feels good and feels real even if it is from a fantasy. These eyes will soon be radiating happiness and safety. I hope and I pray.

"Felicia, over here! I saved you a mat next to me!"

Beth is my bff. She and I are very different, she's a risk taker and I, very conservative. We complement each other they say. There's nothing more that Beth wants for me than to let loose occasionally and have a romantic tryst, so I have yet to tell her that I've been fantasizing about a guy. I'll tell her after yoga when we go for coffee.

Its 120 degrees in here! Holy hotness! Thinking to myself... it cannot get any hotter in here and then as I stretch my legs over my arms and it became much hotter. The mere thought of wrapping my legs around Jake Brown made me quiver, nearing the chills in this hot mess. That's what I am, a hot mess.

"Focus Felicia! Breathe," bantering to myself. The class finally ended and Beth and I took to the showers and headed over to Joe's Diner for coffee. I was in quiet revelation and Beth took notice.

"Hey girl, you haven't said a word. Is work bothering you?"

"Beth, I'm in trouble."

"Felicia, you don't get in trouble. What's going on?"

"Don't make fun of me Beth but I'm fantasizing over this guy I don't even know."

"What do you mean? You don't know him? It's about fucking time you fantasize about someone, tell me more."

"Remember that meeting I had to go to last week in regards to the Bishop kids? As their social worker we had to have an investigation of sorts due to the accusations that Kayla had been throwing around. So, he was there. He's the new investigator for Social Services. I wasn't even introduced to him. I just overheard his name. I can't get him out of my mind Beth. I know it's stupid but there's something about him."

"What does he look like? Is he hot? Is he single? Will you see him again? Oh my god, I'm so excited for you Felicia! It's about time you find someone to pine over after that psycho David."

"Yes, he is hot! Oh hell is he hot. He is a dreamy replacement for that old, crotchety investigator we had before. He is tall, about 6 foot 2 inches is my guess because he is tall like your dad. I actually compared him to your dad."

"Gross Felicia."

"Not in that way, although your father is handsome as all get out. He has shimmering green-blue eyes; my guess is if he's wearing blue they would mirror the ocean. His hair is thick with a slight wave and his jaw line is wanton."

"Look at you girl, you are all wet in the panties. You need to get laid and be dirty for once in your life. Felicia this is your time. Does this tall, hot, dreamy guy have a name?"

"Jake Brown."

"Sounds strong and I can hear you moaning his name... Jake, Oh Jake."

"Shut up Beth! I don't even know him."

"But you want to and that's the important thing. Now it's time to figure out how you'll see him again."

"I have another meeting but I'm not sure he'll be there. But... he has to contact me at some point because I'm the social worker; he'll need me for the investigation."

In realizing this, my whole body feels numb and tingly.

"This is perfect Felicia. You'll have to spend time with him and he'll have to question you, then you can question him."

"Beth, funny. For the first time in my life I feel alive. This morning I looked in the mirror and looked pretty to myself. Those demons weren't looking back at me and the voices weren't there."

"Felicia, you're beautiful. You always have been, inside and out. The past is over and those memories need to fade away. You have to allow them to. If you don't, you'll never fall in love again and you'll never feel loved. But, more importantly, you'll never have hot sex, leg shaking orgasms and the yearning for more."

"Beth, I laid in bed this morning thinking about everything I would do to him and what I would like for him to do to me, that's a start. I don't know what's different about him but it's a need to have him."

In the past three years I hadn't even entertained the idea of meeting a guy, let alone having sex.

"Enough about me how are things with you and Jim? Is he spending less time going through his briefs or more time going through yours?"

"Oh, he's spending time in both briefs but I'm happy and I actually think he's my forever. Who would have thought that I, Beth Kramer would want to settle down? I sure as hell never saw it coming."

"I'm happy for you Beth. Jim is lucky guy to have you in his corner, supporting him through the flack he gets for defending the bad guys."

"It's funny Felicia, at first when he was defending that sick bastard for the double homicides, I didn't think I could handle it or respect him. However, I have to say, working in the firm has taught me a lot about justice and that both sides need representation. He's good at what he does and it turns me on to see him in action."

"Do you think he'll ever switch sides, maybe prosecutor? He's such a kind and gentle man I can't even picture him feisty and dominant in a courtroom but his record speaks volumes."

"Funny you should ask he's actually setting up interviews with the District Attorney's office. As much as he loves his job, I know that it makes it hard when one of the bad guys gets off and he knows they're guilty, you know. So, keep your fingers crossed. Oh and he is very much dominant, if you know what I mean."

We both laughed but I didn't want details and Beth is good at TMI!

"If he goes to the District Attorney's office, how will it feel not working together?"

"I'm actually hoping he does. I think working in the

same office can be tough some times, mostly because I'm the Paralegal investigator and he isn't always happy with what I can't prove. I think it will be great for both of us to work separately."

"Well Beth, I'm praying he gets the position and you can both have separate careers. You are so lucky; he loves you so much and has no qualms about saying so. Although, you never gave him a choice not to love you."

"Girlfriend, I've always told you, you have to take risks in life and I dove into him head first. No pun intended. Now, I will say it again, if you don't take risks Felicia, you will never know what could have been. So this Jake Brown, go after him if you want him. He will be luckiest man to have you."

"You know, I think I'm finally ready to move forward. I think it's is time for me to live. Let's get out of here; I think they're going to kick us out anyway for taking the booth for coffee this long."

"Felicia, please listen to me before we leave. What happened to you was not your fault. You didn't deserve it. That fucker is the sick bastard and he can't hurt you anymore. Forget the things he did and said and reclaim your life. But have a life that is living for more than the foster kids, more than the system. Create a life that brings you joy and excitement and let those scars be a reminder to you of how strong you are and how lucky you are to be alive. You have a second chance and I know it's hard for you but you need to start living and stop hiding from the opposite sex."

"Beth, you're right and something about Jake's eyes spoke safety and comfort to me and I think I'm finally ready to take that risk. Thank you for always being there for me and for pushing me even when I sometimes don't want to be. If I make an ass of myself I'm blaming you though."

"I'll take the blame but once he sets eyes on you he will be smitten. Let's get out of here."

I love Beth, she is a great friend but not only that, she makes me want to move forward. I don't have to live in fear. I don't have to look over my shoulder any longer. David isn't every guy and every guy isn't David.

Today is about change and putting the past behind me, I'm moving forward with freedom and confidence. I have to do this in order for my mind to accept. I have to relive it one more time and then bury it. I have to see it for what it was and let the guilt and blame I have put upon myself go.

David and I went to college together at Northeastern University in Boston. When I met him, he was kind and caring and we became friends. We had a class together and we became study buddies. We spent a lot of time together hanging out, in and out of class. One night, we were at a party and we both had a bit too much to drink and our truths came out. He went first and told me he was in love with me and I reiterated the same to him.

From that moment on, we were a couple. We were happy, we had fun and then he began to change. He became possessive, followed my every move when I wasn't with him. He became accusatory of me playing around with other guys, which was the farthest from the truth. He began to drink more and go to class less.

I tried to talk to him several times and reassure him there was nobody else. He didn't listen, instead he called me a lying whore and raised his hand to me for the first time. I was helpless. I loved him and I didn't understand. I forgave him because he was drunk and he promised it wouldn't happen again.

Finding Home

Things were good for a short while and then after drinking; he started telling me no guy would ever want me because I wasn't pretty. He told me I was just average, nothing special. He said I was a throw away and nobody wanted me. I started to believe the horrible things he said to me.

I sat him down to talk and told him that I thought he should find someone prettier than me and better since he thought I wasn't good enough for him or any other guy. I told him that it was over. I couldn't be treated this way anymore and he begged me not to go.

He promised things would be better and he wouldn't hurt me anymore or call me names. He promised he would make it up to me. I told him it was too late for that, the "I'm Sorry" had no meaning anymore. He begged, pleaded and used all the lines he could have, but I walked away. I was smart enough to have our talk outside in the courtyard where other people were. He would never do anything in public as he had that macho, nice guy image to uphold. He is the big-time Boston attorney's son.

Shaken up for sure and my heart crumbling not only because he was my friend first but he was my lover and I loved him with all of me until year two of our relationship when he changed into the drunk devil.

A few days passed and he didn't show up for class,

which I was happy about. His friends told me he left campus. Relief filled me. Maybe he accepted it and realized he can't treat people like that and expect them to stick around. I felt lighter knowing he wasn't here.

I worked at a café across campus a couple nights a week. Thursday nights I worked until close. It was a dark and dreary night; it had been raining for the past two days. There weren't many people out because of the weather as most people walked when they went anywhere. I locked up and went outside as I had called a cab because it was pouring. Standing by the front door of the café, under the awning, I had an eerie feeling someone was watching me. I looked left and then right and I didn't see anyone. I thought I was being paranoid. I walked closer to the sidewalk as I saw the cab approaching about three traffic lights away.

As I got to the sidewalk, he grabbed me from behind. I felt something poking into my back and heard the words, "Don't you dare say a word. I will kill you right here on the street." I didn't say a word. I knew the voice and I think for me, it made it worse. I could smell the stale liquor on his breath. He threw me into his car and locked all the doors, still pointing the gun at me. I was numb and I said nothing. I'm not sure I knew how to speak with a gun pointing at me.

He blindfolded me and began to drive. David was

rambling on how if he can't have me nobody will. This was his time with me and I will no longer be able to walk away! I kept quiet and the blindfold began to soak from my tears. The fear inside of me was like a pressure cooker ready to explode. I was trapped, beginning to feel very claustrophobic. The anxiety increased as his words went through me like a thorn from a rose. He's going to kill me that was the only thing I knew.

He drove for what seemed like forever and the car came to an abrupt stop. It was still raining and getting very late in the night. He got out of the car pulling me out with him. He held my hand so tight; I could almost feel the bones cracking. He pushed the pistol into my back as he led me to a building. He unlocked the door and threw me inside as I stumbled to the ground. It smelled of dampness and wood—very musty.

He screamed at me, "Get up you whore!"

My voice finally came alive and I asked, "Why are you doing this David? Let's talk and maybe we can work this out, I still love you."

I was desperate. I would say anything for him not to hurt me. I knew he would hurt me in the end. My gut was screaming the truth to me.

"Felicia, we're going to work this out all- right. You are

mine forever and I'm going to make sure of that."

"David, can you take the blindfold off? I want to see you. You're drunk you don't mean any of this."

He took the blindfold off and tied it in my mouth and around my head. He then got coarse rope and tied my hands and then tied each leg up with them straddled. I could no longer say a word, but I could see him and his eyes were filled with rage and danger. I wish I didn't ask for the blindfold to be off. This was not the same David I fell madly in love with. He was once so gentle and had the kindest heart but now he is a demon.

He then pushed me onto a bed, which was as hard as a rock. My heart was pounding out of my chest, the gun so visible to me and now he has taken out a knife. My heart was going to burst. Terror was here. I'm looking right into its eyes.

I lay there, praying to god for forgiveness for him and to help me get away. I prayed that in the end at least he would be caught and for him to never be able to do this to anyone again. I found myself accepting the fact I was going to die but I prayed I wouldn't.

His hand slithered up my body and he ripped my shirt off. I felt the buttons pop off and saw the shiny silver knife coming closer to me. He began at my neck with the knife and went slowly down to my breast. Kissing them and sliding the blade over my areola. He was moaning with pleasure while he sucked my nipples and then he bit down hard, sending pain through my body and catching my breath in my throat.

"These are mine Felicia and when I'm done with you, nobody will ever want to touch them. They will be my possession. "

Defenseless and limp I lie there on this hard bed at his mercy and there's not a damn thing I can do about it. I manage to moan and move my head and he bellowed out…

"You left me Felicia! This is your fault! You made me do this! You're the cause and don't you ever forget it. You will pay for what you did to me. I don't want to hear another fucking sound out of you Bitch!"

He put the knife and the gun down and ripped my bottoms off. He picked the knife back up, cut my panties off and grazed the blade over my pubic area.

I wished at this moment the blindfold was still on. I didn't want to see every step he took in my torture. Nobody will ever find me wherever I am. There's no screaming because I'm bound and gagged. This is it for me. My life is over.

"I'm going to fuck you so hard Felicia. I'm going to make your insides scream in pain; this is what you did to me. It is all your fault. Your sweet pussy is mine forever. You will be damaged goods."

He's going to rape me. He ground his hardness into me and thrust so hard I thought I would pass out and I wish I would. He stared into my eyes and he looked like he was enjoying himself. The pain he was causing me was giving him pleasure. Who the hell is this guy? He looked right through my soul.

"This pussy will never feel love again. I will be the last that ever gets into your hole! Remember this you fucking, disgusting bitch."

After he released himself inside of me, he took the knife and inserted it in me. I was numb down there from his deep and rough penetration. I could feel dripping down my leg but I wasn't sure if it was blood or his cum.

"You like it don't you whore, this sharp, hard object inside of you. Let's try this one. You'll like this better I'm sure it has a much bigger barrel, you like it big don't you. "

He removed the knife and replaced it with the pistol. He was going to shoot me in my vagina. What a sick and twisted bastard. Just take me now God, please spare me from this torture that was all I could think. He was laughing as the tears were pouring down my face as he was pushing the gun deeper inside of me.

He finally took the gun out and came back with the knife. He began to carve his name on my chest. Each time the tip broke the skin I felt more and more out of it. He stopped briefly to guzzle some vodka. I wished he would pour some on me; maybe it would help numb the pain.

He got back on top of me and began to carve a V. Praying he would stop with the E and not spell DAVID. He was moaning and enjoying this too much to be sane. I was beginning to feel very dizzy and lightheaded and he noticed my demeanor. He saw that I was close to losing consciousness so he began to wake me right up with his hand and slap me in the face. Then he took his fist and punched me so hard in the face and the last thing I remember was darkness. When I awoke, it was light out, that much I could see as the sun was shining through the shades. He was gone.

I looked down as far as I could and I could see blood, dried blood. I had no idea how long I had been out for. Perhaps it was better this way. This was my time to escape. I had to find a way to jimmy myself out of these ropes.

I began to wiggle my wrists in desperate hope to loosen the ties. I did this for what seemed like hours. Meanwhile banging against the headboard praying someone would hear me. My strength was no more but I had to give it one last try. As hard as I could muster, I was able to loosen one hand and get out from under the rope. I then undid the other hand and went to the blindfold that had been tying my mouth shut. It was covered in blood.

My mouth was so sore to match the rest of my body. I managed to reach down to untie my feet and saw more blood and empty syringes lying next to me. He must have been giving me shots of something while I was unconscious. That's why it was now light out; he drugged me to stay asleep.

My clothes lay on the floor, some sliced and ripped to shreds. My bare body was weak and damaged and I had an atrocious headache. I crawled off the bed and slithered my way to the bathroom. The floor was of broken tiles, there was a tub, a sink and a toilet that were filthy. I pulled myself up to the toilet and began to pee. It burned and felt like clumps were coming out of me. I looked in the toilet and it was filled with blood. He cut my insides. I'm going to die, this I know to be true.

There was a towel in the bathroom that was covered in mold but that was my only means to cover my body and escape this place. I wrapped the towel around me and started to crawl to the door to get out. My purse was on the floor but my phone was gone. It dawned on me that I have the Find My Phone App on my phone and a glimmer of hope came that maybe someone could track it and at least find David so he couldn't come back to finish me off.

With every ounce of energy I had, I opened the door. It was what I would normally think beautiful outside with so many trees and dirt roads leading out of where I was. I had never been here before. It wasn't beautiful to me now, it was hell on earth. I was able to get on my feet and take small steps outside where I was relieved to see a cabin down the road a bit with a car parked outside. With the moldy towel wrapped around my sluggish body, I gingerly walked to the cabin. It took me what felt like hours to reach the door to knock.

I knocked on the door, once, twice and finally on the third try an older lady came to the door. She opened the door and her face fell white at the sight of me.

"I need help!"

"Oh dear, you need to get to a hospital. I'm going to call the police and the ambulance, stay right here."

"Can I please come in; I don't know if he's still out here. My name is Felicia."

"Yes, Come in and let me get you something to put on you while we wait for the police. I'm calling them now. Put this blanket over you for a minute and I'll get you some clothes while we wait."

"Thank you. I'm sorry to bother you but I'm so happy you're here."

"The police are on their way. What happened to you Felicia? Who did this to you? Can I get you some water?"

The poor lady didn't know what to do or say. I was getting increasingly groggier.

"Yes, water would be great and my ex boyfriend did this to me."

I began to sob, my body went into shakes and I could not stop it. The nice lady brought me a robe, it was long and soft and it felt much better being covered up. I drank the water almost in one sip. The lady stared at me and kept her distance from me as if I was some kind of monster. I didn't much care though she was calling for help. I started to spin and I felt myself fading. I woke up in the hospital with bandages over my head, on my arms, my feet and my chest. I was hooked up to machines and IV's and as I opened my eyes, there were two police officers there, a male and a female.

FELICA & OFFICER CAROL

Officer Carol came to my bedside and put her hand on my arm. I looked at her through the slits of my eyes and she gave me a comforting look. She asked the other officer to leave the room so we could have a moment. He did.

"Hi Felicia, I'm Officer Carol. You've been hurt bad but I want you to know you're safe here; we have police all around and outside your door. We are going to get the bastard that did this to you. There's some questions I need to ask you. I only have your first name, could you tell me your last name please?"

"Westfield is my last name."

"Felicia, do you have any family we can contact?"

"No, my mother died when I was seven and my father is a useless drunk and I don't even know where he is. I was in and out of foster homes until I was eighteen, so no family to contact. There is someone though, my best friend, Beth Kramer."

I gave her Beth's phone number.

"Okay, I'll give her a call, would she have known you

were missing?"

"Yes, we talk everyday no matter what. She lives in Boston and goes to Boston University. How long have I been gone? What day is it today?

"We're thinking at least a week or more. From your injuries and the lack of nutrition, the doctors narrowed it down a bit. Today is Saturday."

"Well, he took me Thursday night from the café, so it's only been two days."

"More like a week and two days Felicia. You had drugs in your system that made you sleep. At a very quick glance, he left you at that cabin the day before you woke up. The drugs in your system were given often, therefore, he had to have been the one giving them to you. I'm so sorry. I know this isn't easy."

"Is there a mirror that I can look at?"

"I'm not sure you want to do that Felicia, you're pretty banged up."

"I do. Please can you get me a mirror, I need to see."

She put a mirror up to my eyes and I didn't recognize the foreign object in front of me. My left eye swollen and displaying multiple colors of black, brown, orange, yellow and a hint even of green. My right eye was not as bad but bruises took residence upon my entire face.

My nose is swollen and my lips had slits in them. My head is bandaged and I have no idea what is underneath there, except that my hair was shaven to the middle of my head. I had Officer Carol open my gown and let me look at my chest. Nausea took over and I vomited in my hospital bed. There it was, carved from my left breast to my right. DAVID. He had carved a line from my breast to just under my navel and there was an arrow pointing down and an X.

My legs and arms looked okay comparatively, lots of bruises and cuts from the rope and his grip. I am ugly. I am scarred and I look like a freak. The words ran through my head, "This is your fault, you made me do this."

"This is my entire fault. I deserved it; I never should have left him. He took everything from me and I only have myself to blame."

Now sobbing. He might as well have killed me I'm revolting now. Scarred for life.

"Felicia, this is not your fault. You certainly didn't deserve this. This person is a crazy son of a bitch. He tortured you, raped you and he's going to pay for this! Mark my words. He is a sick bastard and none of this is your fault. Nobody deserves this!"

"Do you know where he is? He has my cell phone and I have the tracking App on it, you can find him that way. Please find him and lock him up! He needs help."

"We have an all out bulletin out for him; we have officers looking into your cell phone now. I know it wasn't easy to share what happened to you Felicia but it will help us put him behind bars. I think right now, you need to get some rest. Here is my card, please call me with any questions. You're safe here; we won't stop until we find him. Get some rest."

"Thank you."

Once the door closed, everything in my being let go. The floodgates opened and I was scouring my body of his assault. I will never be able to show my body to another man ever. He ruined me. I will never be able to look at myself and not remember. I laid my head down while I sobbed myself to sleep.

Awoken by machines beeping, the doctors ran in. My blood pressure was dropping; I was foggy but now partially awake. They lifted the blankets and the bed was soaked in blood. I was bleeding from my vagina. They gave me a shot in my arm and I vaguely remember them saying, "You're going to be okay, we have to get you to surgery."

The next morning I woke to find Beth by my bedside. I could see the fright in her eyes and she held my hand gently.

"Hey Beth, I'm so glad to see you."

"Oh Felicia, I'm so sorry this happened to you. These doctors are taking good care of you. You're going to be okay, I promise. I was so worried about you."

"Will I? I hurt, everywhere, worse than before."

At that moment, I tried to move a bit, opened up my gown and saw heavy bandages on my chest and a new bandage down my belly. Confused. I looked at Beth with bewilderment.

"I'm so sorry Felicia; they had to perform an emergency hysterectomy. The knife cut some organs and you started to hemorrhage. They also did some skin grafts to cover the carvings on your skin."

"Oh."

Clearly in shock, my reaction was null. The doctor came in, explained everything to me and assured me that I would be okay with time. She was nice. Dr. Sandy she called herself. She sat with me when Beth had to leave and held my hand. A very kind woman. Not old at all but she felt like a mother figure.

After three long weeks in the hospital, I was released. With healing scars and a broken soul, I was on my own again. They caught David and he was arrested for kidnapping, felonious sexual assault and a few other things. He was arraigned and held without bail until his trial. At least I was safe going back to my apartment.

Beth got me settled back in and stayed with me for a few days before she had to go back for her finals before graduation. I wouldn't be attending finals or graduation. I wasn't ready for being in public. The scars were so new and I couldn't handle the questions or the attention.

Beth had arranged with the Dean of Northeastern to take my finals via computer and just have my diploma mailed to me and that is what I did. Now, I have relived every bloody moment of that horrific ordeal. I really believe I may be ready to move on. David got 6 years in prison, not long enough in my opinion but I hoped he would change and get help. He had a top attorney from his father's firm. Only the best for David, maybe that's why he became deranged, always used to getting everything he wanted.

I never saw the sign until he started drinking. I guess that's when his true colors came out. Perhaps I was blinded by his charm and his attention to me before the drinking began. It was if a switch went on and he was a different person. Cruel, insulting, apologetic, and unpredictable. He did win in the end. Nobody will ever want to touch me again or make love to me. I'm tainted.

After the hours of reflection today, I'm exhausted but excited. As many emotions doing so caused, I feel I have released so much anger and self-blame. As I stared in the mirror, there were scars, yes but as Beth said, they represent my strength and courage. I am strong; I am woman, a survivor.

For the first time, I feel worthy of love and less afraid to be intimate emotionally and physically. The smile will shine on my face more now. I want it and I choose it. Jake Brown will never notice me if I don't smile. Just thinking of him, delivers chills and fire at the same time throughout my body. An anxiety I never felt before. If there can be good anxiety I'm feeling it.

After two and half years of therapy, cognitive and sexual therapy, I can feel again. I know I can feel want and desire. Dr. Linda Shattuck made me confront myself in a way I never had before. In order to determine if I would have any stimulation in the down below region, she gave me many exercises to do at home to myself. She taught me how to masturbate. It was uncomfortable at first and it took some real time but after daily kiegel exercises and getting to know my own hands and a vibrator, I was able to get the sensation back. I can reach climax and it feels great just knowing he didn't take that from me.

I want a man to feel me, to make me want him, to show him that he turns me on. David didn't take that away from me forever, only temporarily. I will feel pleasure again from a man and I will give him pleasure.

Wow, this is truly awesome. I haven't thought anything remotely like this. I'm twenty-six years old, I have lost so much time and Jake Brown's eyes have opened mine. Whether or not we ever meet, he has changed me already. I owe him and I don't even know him.

I have an early appointment to check in with the Bishop kids in the morning. I'll be taking them out of the house today so I can talk with them. I will take them to the park and for ice cream. There's Kayla, Joey and Adam. Kayla is ten, Joey is nine and Adam is four. They have been in foster care nearing six months. Their mother is a drug addict and there are three different fathers who are all druggies as well.

The foster mom said Kayla is accusing one of the other foster kids, Daniel, who is sixteen years old of touching her inappropriately. Since she brought this to our attention, Daniel has been put in respite until the investigation is complete. When I take the foster kids out, I like to take them out together. Especially these three as they are very anxious. They have separation anxiety from each other.

These three young kids woke up to find their house on fire and their mom passed out. They lost everything. The mom was cooking something, she left the kitchen to drink, shoot up and then passed out and the pan caught on fire.

They lived in a mobile home so it was quite small. The fire went to the cabinets, then to the curtains and it spread from there.

The kids woke up from the smoke and couldn't find their mom because she was on the floor and the smoke was thick. They ran outside, holding one another's hands and got a neighbor. The firefighter came and pulled the mom out, she was alive but clearly unconscious.

She went to the hospital and the kids were put into foster care that night. They lost everything, which wasn't too much to speak of. Adam's blanket dropped while they were trying to get out of the house and most of it burned. He was screaming for his blanket and the firefighter cut out the burned part and gave it to him. He can't sleep without it.

When their mom regained consciousness, she never

asked about the kids. She was insisting to leave the hospital and go to her new boyfriend's house. That didn't happen; she was arrested at her bedside for neglect. These kids have been through the ringer and if someone is touching Kayla, I will find out and it will be stopped.

What a glorious morning to wake up and hear the birds singing for the first time in years. I feel rested and ready to conquer the day. I got up, showered and put on a light pink blouse with white pants. I applied make up lightly and I did my hair in a French braid.

I went to the kitchen, made a cup of coffee from my Keurig, sat and drank the French Vanilla Blend on my porch just staring out at the nature that I never knew was so peaceful before now. I grabbed a blueberry muffin and went out to my car to take the Bishop kids to the park. When I got in my car, I thought it would be nice to have a picnic in the park. I ran back inside and made some PB & J sandwiches and apple slices and of course, gummy bears that I always had on hand to bring to them. The three kids love them.

Driving over to pick up the kids, every little thing looked brighter to me. I finally feel hope and a new start coming my way. I'm hearing the sounds of the traffic, which is awkwardly pleasant to me. I feel the energy that is buzzing around me. It has just hit me how I have blocked everything out for the past three years. No more. Look out world because I have re-entered!

I'm here at the Foster home to pick up the three kids. As I walk up the walkway, I notice for the first time the impeccably manicured landscape. I never noticed it before. I was always just focused on the kids and seeing them. Breathtaking! The house is not a house, it's an estate, sitting on three acres of land with fruit trees and gardens. The Monroe family couldn't have kids of their own so they have dedicated their lives to foster parenting. I wish I had been put in their care when I was younger. Cindy Monroe is sweet, tolerant and dedicated to her foster kids. As caring and as lovely as she is, she has given up some of her past foster kids because of issues. Her husband Harold comes from a wealthy family and when his parents passed away he inherited millions.

"Hi Felicia, come on in. The kids are excited to go out with you today. Can I get you something to drink?"

"Cindy thank you but I'm all set. Do you have a second before the kids come down?

"Of course. Is this about Kayla," Cindy asked.

"Yes. As you know we're investigating the allegations against Daniel but I wanted to get your thoughts on it. Has Kayla opened up to you at all?"

"Kayla is a storyteller. You know that. Daniel has some problems. He was abused himself. It's possible but I'm very in tuned with what goes on around here. I think I would know that. I think Kayla is looking for some attention and she knows that Daniel was abused that's why he's in foster care. Moreover, I think she has a bit of a crush on him because he's older. He doesn't feel the same way about her, so I think she's made up this lie."

"So Cindy, you think she is making this up?"

"Honestly, I do. She hasn't been herself lately. I think she needs the attention and by her making up the story, she is getting it, you're here now to take them out, and you know how much she adores you. It's working in her favor, don't you see?"

"Well, we have to take these things seriously, regardless if they are true or not. We have to look out for each child. The Bishop kids are very special to me and I will do anything to keep them safe. I know you want the same."

"Of course I do Felicia; I just don't want people to think things like that happen in my home."

The kids came down the spiral staircase.

"Hey Adam. How are you champ?

"Do you have gummy bears, Ms. Felicia?"

"I sure do kiddo. I need a hug before you have any though."

"Yup."

"Hey Kayla, hey Joey, we're going to the park and going to have a picnic. Does that sound good?"

"Sounds good to us."

I hear Kayla mutter something under her breath.

"Okay, let's get going. Cindy I'll have them back in a few hours. Enjoy your day and think about what we talked about."

"I will. Kids behave for Ms. Felicia. This is a special treat today. Come over and give me a hug."

The hesitation of Kayla was undeniable. She didn't want to hug Cindy at all. It made me curious. Adam ran right up to her and hugged her and Joey stood back and wouldn't go to her either.

We got to the park and it wasn't crowded yet. The swings were their favorite and the merry go round that made me want to throw up.

"C'mon kids, let's race to the swings and see who can swing the highest. Don't worry Adam, I'll push you."

We raced to the swings and they all hopped on. Kayla and Joey were always competing with each other; today I hope Kayla goes the highest. She looks so sad and frightened. I pushed Adam and he was singing and smiling with every pump of the swing. Joey went the highest and Kayla jumped off in midair and ran behind a tree.

The tree was a few feet away from the swings, so I asked Joey to keep an eye on Adam while I went and talked with Kayla. They were in my sight so it was okay.

"Kayla honey, what is it? Did Joey going the highest upset you that much?"

"No, it just hurts so much every time I move on the swing."

"Where does it hurt Kayla?"

"My privates."

"Why do your privates hurt honey? Did you fall and hurt yourself? Is it Daniel?"

"No, it's not Daniel. It never was Daniel. They told me to say it was him. Daniel is my friend. Daniel would never hurt me."

"Okay honey. It's going to be okay. Than if it isn't Daniel who is it? Who told you to say it was Daniel?"

"I can't say. They told me if I did I would never see Joey or Adam again."

"Kayla, can you tell what this person did to you?"

"Miss. Felicia, I'm scared."

"I know honey but I will protect you, I promise."

"Papa Harold visits me at night while I'm sleeping. I woke up one night and he was naked in bed with me. His pee pee was touching me. It hurt against my leg because it was hard and he was pushing it into my leg. It wasn't like Adam's; I know I used to have to change his diapers. I wasn't even sure if it was his pee pee. I asked him why he was naked and he told me because this is the best way to sleep. I asked him what that hard thing was that was hurting me and he said it was his penis and that's what it was supposed to do when he saw a beautiful girl. He said I was his beautiful girl."

"What happened next Kayla? Take your time honey."

"He pulled up my nighty and rubbed his pee pee on my belly and I didn't like it! It was weird and scary looking."

"Then he kissed my mouth and bit my lip. I cried Felicia. I told him he was not supposed to do this to me. He said it was because he loved me and he was the daddy I never had. He said that Mama Cindy likes him to show the kids he loves them because he's not around a lot."

My mouth dropped and my stomach was doing somersaults. Harold the well-respected man in town is a pedophile.

"What happened next Kayla?"

"He told me I was special and not to tell anyone because it was our little secret. His mouth tasted gross Felicia... like poop. He then got up and left. Mama Cindy was waiting for him outside the door. I saw them kissing in the hallway."

"Was that the only time he came in your room?"

"No, he keeps coming in while I'm sleeping and waking me up. Last night he came in again."

She began to sob. My heart broke for her. I took her hand and held it in mine and assured her this was not going to happen again.

"Kayla, what happened last night?"

"He woke me up and gave me gummy bears. He told me how pretty I was and how much he loved me. His pee pee was sticking straight up and he told me it was time for him to show me how much he loved me. I told him he was hurting me and he covered my mouth with his hand and told me to not make a sound that I would wake up Adam."

She kept looking at the ground and didn't want to tell me anymore. She wanted to go to the Merry Go Round with her brothers.

"Kayla, let's go on the Merry Go Round and we'll talk in a bit okay. You know I can't go on it. I will push it."

She smiled at me and grabbed my hand and I helped her up. Joey and Adam were having loads of fun in the huge sandbox. Building castles with the sand toys.

"Hey boys, let me push you on the Merry Go Round."

"Yeah! Ms. Felicia are you coming on with us," Joey asked with excitement.

"No boys, it makes me feel yucky. I'll push you though."

"Okay chicken," said Joey.

"You got me, I'm a chicken."

We all laughed even Kayla. They got on and I walked around and made it spin. Even that made me feel wobbly but I had to do it for the kids. They were laughing, howling, and loving the ride. These kids just want love and simple pleasures. They had never been to a park before I brought them the first time and it has become our place.

"Who's hungry?"

The kids all yelled out, "Me, Me, Me!"

"We have to go to the bathhouse first to wash all that dirt off your hands. Adam and Joey, you two are filthy."

They both laughed and we all walked to the stone building that had the bathrooms. Kayla told the boys to make sure to really scrub their hands and wipe them after. She was a like a mother to them. Kayla and I went to the girl's room and whoever was done first would wait outside the door for the other.

There were two stalls in the bathroom. We both shut our doors and I heard the stream hit the water but I also heard whimpering from Kayla.

"Kayla, are you okay? Is something wrong?"

"It hurts… it really hurts."

"Kayla I'm coming in. There's nobody else in here but

you and me, okay. Unlock the door."

She unlocked the door and I walked in to the tiny stall and nearly lost my breath. There were specs of blood running down Kayla's leg and her thighs were bruised. She looked at me through her tear smothered eyes and said, "Help me Ms. Felicia, I'm bleeding. Am I going to die?"

"Kayla, oh honey, I'm right here. No, you are not going to die, I promise. Let me wipe you up and we are going to go to my friend Dr. Sandy, okay. She will fix you right up and you'll be like new again, okay?"

"Will I get a shot? I don't like shots; shots make you not know where you are and act weird."

"No honey, no shots today. Did you know shots are not all bad; they keep you from getting sick? The shots that a doctor gives you sometimes don't feel good but they can keep you healthy. "

"Ms. Felicia, will you stay with me at the doctor?"

"I won't leave your side. Let's go have that picnic quick and we will bring the boys to my office while we go see my friend Dr. Sandy. Okay?"

"Okay, but why can't they go home?"

"Kayla… Papa Harold did something very wrong and neither of you are going back there."

"But he said he loved me and he told me not to tell anyone or I wouldn't see Joey or Adam again. I can't be away from my brothers, they're all I have. He's going to take Joey and Adam away now that I told!"

She started to cry and her hands began to shake at the thought of her losing her brothers. I'm trying with all my might to hold back the tears. I bent down to her level, held her hands and said, "Papa Harold and Mama Cindy do love you, but what he did to you was wrong. Nobody touches your privates, nobody. You did the right thing by telling me. You are not in trouble. I promise you that. He won't be able to touch you ever again. He will not be able to take Joey and Adam from you either. Don't worry that pretty little head of yours."

We walked out of the bathroom and the boys were waiting patiently for us. We walked over under the tree and set out the blanket and the picnic I had prepared. The boys were sticking the gummy bears in their PB & J sandwiches and Kayla was barely touching her food. After we were done eating, I told the boys that I had to bring them to my office because Kayla wasn't feeling well and I had to take her to the doctor.

"Can I have your gummy bears if you're sick Kayla," Joey asked.

"You can have them but you have to share with Adam

and make sure he doesn't choke."

"Okay thanks. Do I have to share the reds one with him?"

"Adam doesn't like the red ones anyways, just give him some Joey."

"Thanks Kayla, I love you."

"I love you too Joey!"

Kayla and Joey both had watering eyes, as if they both knew what the other was thinking.

We gathered all our things and walked to the car. Kayla is holding one hand and Adam, the other. Joey was carrying the things like a grown man. We drove to my office and the boys were excited because they liked my colleague Erin. I went to speak with Erin and quickly explained the situation. She came out of her office and went to the boys. She told them they could watch a movie in her office and draw. They loved to draw.

"Yeah! Miss Erin I'm going to draw you a picture," Joey said.

"Joey, I can't wait and Adam are going to draw me a picture too?"

"No, but I'll give you a hug."

Adam was a love bug. He was so cute and loveable. Always ready to give a hug. Adam was a precious little boy.

"Well, that's even better Adam. Come over here. I got a hug for you too."

It was a quiet ride to Dr. Sandy's office. Kayla was scared as well as me. This poor little girl, defenseless, confused and violated. Shit, its making me have flashbacks. Go Away! Stop!

Erin called Dr. Sandy and told her we were coming. We arrived at the hospital where Dr. Sandy's office was and I could see the fear envelope Kayla's face.

"Honey, it will all be okay. No shots."

"I'm going to get in trouble. I don't want to get a spanking again. Do we have to go Miss Felicia?"

"Yes, we do and you are not in trouble. You didn't do anything wrong, in fact you only did things right. This is not your fault. You are not in trouble. I promise."

We got in the elevator to the second floor where the Ob/Gyn office is. Dr. Sandy is my gynecologist. I opened the heavy oak door to the office and there were pregnant women sitting in the waiting room. For a split second, I was reminded how I will never come to this office pregnant. Sadness crept over me and then I looked down at Kayla, shaking and pale. This isn't about me; it's about this poor, innocent girl.

"Felicia Westfield to see Dr. Sandy please."

"Yes, come right back. She's waiting for you. You must be Kayla. I have a lollipop for you. Here you go."

"Thank you," she replied.

The woman brought us to a room with pink walls and loads of pictures of babies. Over the table where Kayla will be examined was a mobile of kittens. Kayla loved kitties. I lifted Kayla up on the table and helped her put the gown on. She was silent and trembling.

Dr. Sandy came in the door and looked at me and smiled a smile that was only there to break the fear that was in the room.

"Hi Kayla, I'm Dr. Sandy. I'm a friend of Felicia's. Do you trust Felicia, Kayla?"

"Yes."

"Good, because she trusts me. I've been her doctor for three years and she keeps coming back so that means I don't hurt her, right?"

"I guess so. Am I going to have a shot? Please say no."

"No shots today honey but I am going to look at your privates. I promise you that I will be very gentle and if it hurts I want you tell me right away, okay?"

"Okay."

"Kayla, I want you to lay back and try and relax. Look up at the kittens above you, they are so cute. Right now I'm just going to look and not touch okay?"

"Yup."

"So, how old are you Kayla?"

"I'm ten years old and I have two brothers. I'm the oldest."

"Wow, you are lucky. I don't have any brothers. Do you like having brothers?"

"Yeah, I guess. I don't have a mom or dad though."

"Oh honey, I'm sorry. But you have Felicia and she adores you. She told me so."

"I like her too."

Kayla looked at me and smiled. I grabbed her hand as things were going to get a bit uncomfortable for her.

"Okay Kayla, see this flashlight… I have to turn it on and look at your vagina. It won't hurt. I'm going to use my finger to look too. If it hurts please tell me to stop."

Kayla stared at me the whole time and tears began to trickle down her cheeks.

"I'm right here Kayla. Squeeze my hand if it hurts. Dr. Sandy is going to fix you. You have to lay real still okay?"

"It hurts. Ouchy, it hurts."

"Kayla, can you hang in there a bit longer. I have to use this long Q-tip. You know what a Q-tip is right. They clean your ears and this is the same thing. I am going to clean your privates. Almost done. You are so brave. Much braver than Felicia, she is a chicken."

Kayla smiled and held my hand tighter as she inserted the long Q-tip.

"We are all done. You did great. I'm so proud of you Kayla. I think you deserve an ice cream from Felicia."

"Can we get an ice-cream Miss Felicia? But we have to get one for the boys too. They like the cotton candy kind."

"We will go for ice cream. You earned it. I'm so proud of you. Maybe you can help me not be such a chicken since you're so brave."

"Kayla, Felicia and I are going to go to my office for a minute but my nurse Linda will be here with you. I have to find you a special sticker."

"Okay. I like kitties."

"I'll see what I can do. We'll be right back."

Dr. Sandy and I walked to her office. Once we got there and closed the door, she confirmed that there had been penetration of Kayla's vagina. There was some tearing and she still had some blood coming out. She was raped.

"Sandy, I can't believe anyone would do this to a young girl. Sick bastard. Is there any serious damage?"

"No, she's likely to be sore for a few days but nothing that won't heal, thankfully. I know this is extra hard for you Felicia because of what you went through but know that she will be okay."

A knock on the door sounded. Dr. Sandy got up to open it and welcomed him in the room.

"Come in Jake. I just finished the exam. Jake, this is Felicia Westfield. Felicia this is Jake Brown. He's an investigator for Social Services."

"Ms. Westfield, nice to meet you. I've heard a lot about you."

"Uh hum, nice to meet you too Mr. Brown. Please call me Felicia."

Holy shit, it's him! Right in front of me. He is perfect. Wow, those eyes.

"So Sandy, what do we have here? Is the foster kid sexually abusing Kayla? Please tell me no."

"No, not by the foster kid."

"Thank god."

"Jake, its worse. If it can get any worse. Her foster father raped her. Now, we don't have any DNA yet but from the examination and the tearing she has, this was not a sixteen year old boy."

Jake's vibrant eyes became cloudy with sadness as Dr. Sandy delivered her findings. It was an immediate shift in demeanor.

"Mr. Brown, Kayla told me everything today while at the park. That's why I took her here. I brought her to Sandy because I thought it would be more comfortable for Kayla."

"Please call me Jake. What a sick son of a bitch. Don't people understand what this does to kids? I am sorry ladies this just makes me sick. Do you know if there was more than one violation Sandy?"

"Well, she has bruising on her upper and inner thigh. She has bruises on her arms and her belly along with serious bruising and tears in the vagina. My guess would be that there was more than one violation and perhaps other acts as well."

"Felicia, we need to call the police. Please do not contact the Monroe's; we don't want to tip them off in any way."

"I better get back to Kayla. I'm sure she's wondering if she's in trouble or something, plus I have to bring her to get ice cream."

"That's right Felicia, you need to get her and the boy's ice cream. Go ahead, I think we're done here anyway. You did good Felicia. That little girl is lucky to have you."

"Thanks Sandy and thank you for taking a look at her. I didn't want her in the Emergency Room with some man doctor that would have scared her more. Jake, so nice to meet you. I hope to see you soon."

I cannot believe I just said that. He has got me all in a tussle. I walked out the door and every nerve in my body was tingling. Hope to see you soon, what a fool I just made of myself. I'm nearly hitting on him while we are discussing such a serious issue. He sure does take these cases to heart. It shows a lot about his character.

"Hey Kayla, are you ready for that ice cream at the Crunchy Cone?"

"Yeah, I'm kind of hungry since I didn't eat much lunch."

"Okay kiddo, let's go. Are you feeling okay? That wasn't that bad was it? Sandy's nice right?"

"I'm tired but I think I feel better. I don't know. I didn't like it but Sandy was nice."

We walked down the hall to the elevator swinging hands. Kayla seemed more relaxed. I'm so proud of her bravery and for telling me the truth. Cindy Monroe thinks Kayla's the storyteller, my ass.

Finding Home

We stepped into the elevator, the door was closing and a hand stopped it. Jake stepped in the elevator with us. Holy shit. He is so gorgeous. In a two by four area, I can hear him breathing and I can bet he can see my heart pounding.

"Hey, you must be Kayla. I'm Jake."

"Kayla it's okay. Jake works with me and he's a good guy."

He smiled at me. WOW! He looked right in my eyes and I had the strangest feeling I've known him forever. It was if he just reached into my soul.

"Hi Jake. We're going to get an ice cream at the Crunchy Cone. Do you want to come with us?"

"Hmmm, let me think, I would love to. That's my favorite place."

Well, leave it to a kid to set things up. Kayla has way more courage than I ever will. Thank you Kayla. Jake followed us to the Crunchy Cone. The lines were long. I hope that Kayla will help with conversation. She's less than shy, so I think it will flow okay.

"What's your favorite ice cream Felicia?

"I'm a yogurt kind of girl, so Purple Cow."

"How about you Miss Kayla?"

"Bubblegum. What's yours Jake?"

"I'm a yogurt kind of guy too so Purple Cow for me."

"Oooh you two like the same ice cream."

My heart was pounding and Jake smiled at me with his breathtaking smile. There are parts of him I would like to eat my yogurt off. I have to stop; this is just a kind gesture, him coming along. Nothing more. He probably wants to question Kayla. We are next in line.

"What can I get you sir?"

"I need a bubblegum ice cream cone with a cherry on top for this pretty young lady. A Purple Cow yogurt for this beautiful woman. I will have a scoop of Bubblegum and Purple Cow. Thank you."

"That was very sweet Jake. Thank you."

"Don't thank me; I'm the one who should be thanking you. I'm the envy of all men right now with two beautiful ladies by my side."

"Jake, do you like Ms. Felicia? My teacher at school told me you could always tell if someone likes you by the way they look at you. You look like you like Ms. Felicia."

"Miss Kayla, I think you may be right. You like her right?"

"I sure do."

"If you like her Kayla than I think I do too."

"Okay you two, let's eat our ice cream and we can't forget to order Joey and Adam's."

We sat at the picnic table and ate our ice cream and yogurt. The conversation was easy; of course, Kayla was doing most of the talking. I think she has a crush on Jake Brown too. Jake and I both kept catching the other looking. He made me blush. I wanted badly to grab his hand because it felt right but I didn't.

After we were finished, I went and ordered the boys ice cream. Jake had to go back to the office too so he followed us there.

"Ms. Felicia, do you like Jake? He is wicked cute. I think he likes you."

"Kayla we just met. I think he's nice and don't tell anyone but I think he is wicked cute too."

We laughed. Kayla and I built a bond today that would never be severed. Another tough part when we get to the office. We have to tell the kids they aren't going back to the Monroe's. They will stay tonight in our apartment in the office with Erin and we'll find a good foster home for the three of them.

When we arrived back at the office, Adam was

sleeping and Joey was still drawing pictures for Erin.
At a quick glance at his drawings, they were very
strange. We woke Adam up to eat his ice cream and
he was so happy to have his favorite Cotton Candy.
While they were happily eating, we thought it would be
a good time to tell them they wouldn't be going back
to the Monroe's.

Adam started to cry and said he needed his blanket.
Joey was happy; he gave us a high five. I found this
odd; I thought he liked it there. Then I thought back
to when we were leaving and he wouldn't hug Cindy.
Kayla was more than thrilled.

"Adam, I'll go get your blanket and some clothes for
the three of you. Everything is going to be all-right
kiddos, don't you worry. You are safe and nobody will
hurt you ever again."

"You promise," asked Joey.

"I promise Joey; all the bad times are behind you
now."

I looked up and Jake was standing in the doorway. He
looked at me and smiled. I went out in the hall and
told him that I thought there was more than just Kayla
being abused. After listening at the door he had the
same suspicion.

"I have to go get Adam's blanket and some clothes;

they will stay in the apartment with Erin tonight. I'm glad she is on call tonight, they love her. Thank you for the ice cream. I must run so I can get back before Adam has to go to sleep. I can't believe he fell asleep without his blanket earlier."

"Wait Felicia, I'm coming with you. I don't want you going there by yourself. Who knows how Cindy Monroe will be after her husband was taken into custody."

"Okay, you have a point."

"I'll drive and you can control the radio Felicia. Is that a deal?"

"Deal!"

I never would have expected my day to be in the presence of Mr. Jake Brown. I'm in a car with him and he is oh so sexy, with one hand on the wheel and the other on the shifter. I find myself staring at him and remembering him licking his ice cream. Something about him has awakened every sense of mine. He must have felt me staring at him and he turned and gave me a cute smile.

We arrived at the house and he came around and opened my door for me. What the hell is that? Nobody has ever opened the door for me. As we walked the beautiful walkway with flowers lining it, his hand was on my lower back. It felt good, it felt right. We knocked on the door and there was no answer. We called the office to let them know we were going in. All of the social workers have keys to the houses in case there is an emergency. This is an emergency, Adam needs his blanket.

Jake took the key from me as he noticed my hands were shaking. Little did he know I was shaking from his touch. We stepped inside and called out for Cindy Monroe. There was no answer. Jake was in awe of this mansion. We both walked up the spiral staircase to get to the kid's bedrooms. We went to Adam's room first to get his blanket; it was lying on his bed by his pillow. I grabbed a few things for him to wear out of his dresser. Next, we went to Kayla's room. Her bed was unmade and there was a nightgown on the floor in a ball that had been ripped in half. I looked at Jake and he turned down the covers of her bed and found bloodstains.

"This is now a crime scene. I need to call it in. Grab her some clothes but leave the nightgown where it is. That sick fucking bastard."

While Jake was on the phone with the police, I went to Joey's room. His bed wasn't made either and his teddy bear was half under the pillow and half out. I thought I should bring that to him. As I picked up the pillow to grab the bear, I saw blood on his sheets as well.

"Jake, come here quick, there's blood on Joey's sheets!"

My stomach was churning and I felt as though I would throw up. That son of a bitch did it to him too. That's why Joey was happy to leave there. The people who pass themselves off as "saving" children are violating them.

"Are you okay Felicia?"

"I'm not so sure. How can anyone do this to such innocent kids?"

"Sick, sick minds. Let's just say, he will get his in prison. C'mon, let's wait outside for the police. I think we have seen enough. We'll let them find the rest. Hopefully there isn't anymore."

Jake's eyes shifted again to the same as they were in Dr. Sandy's office. There has to be something behind them. He is affected and he is an ex-cop trained to not react but he's reacting.

"Jake, thank you for coming with me and thank you for being so kind to Kayla today. It helped more than you can imagine."

"Let's just say, I know how she feels. Plus I love kids."

Oh great, he loves kids. We won't go far than. I can't have kids. I wonder what he means that he knows how she feels. We went outside and sat on the front steps. We were both quiet and quite exhausted. The police arrived and Jake did most of the talking. They told us they would take it from here and they would contact us later after their search. Thankfully, they got an emergency warrant.

We drove back to the office and gave the kids their things. I introduced Jake to Adam and Joey. Jake would be talking with Joey in the morning. They seemed to like him too. I gave them all hugs and kisses and Erin promised if there were any issues that she would call me right away.

Jake and I left the apartment and I went to grab the pictures that Joey had drawn. At first glance they were very strange and they may just tell a story. I had to find out. At this point, nothing will surprise me.

Jake was waiting for me by the exit. His eyes gleamed of comfort and safety and his lips looked so soft. His eyes had transformed back to the first time I saw him. My imagination is running wild. I need to go to bed.

"Felicia, are you okay? Can we go somewhere and talk? I know this was a tough day for you."

"I'm okay. Just lots of emotions running in my head but I'm okay. Do you want to come to my place; it's not too far from here? I don't make a habit of asking guys to my apartment but I just don't feel like being surrounded by people. Do you mind?

"That sounds great. I'll follow you."

"Okay. I can't even remember if my place is clean or not so keep your eyes closed until we walk in."

We both chuckled.

FELICIA & JAKE

I opened the door and took a quick glance at the place to see if Jake could open his eyes. The coast was clear, so I let him come in. The day was so long. I couldn't remember if I left my underwear on the floor or something. I live in a studio apartment. You don't make much in money as a social worker but the rewards make up for it.

"Your place is nice Felicia."

"Why thank you Jake. It isn't much but it's as close to home as I can get. It's quiet and the neighbors don't bother me. Can I get you something to drink? I have lemonade, water, diet coke and wine."

"If you'll have a glass of wine with me, I would love one. If not, I'll take lemonade."

"Wine it is. I could use it."

I can't believe he is sitting in my apartment right now on my sofa. My bed is in the same room. This is weird for sure. I wish I could call Beth and ask her what to do. It's been years since I've been alone with a man, not to mention one that is so frieken gorgeous. I poured two glasses of wine and brought it over to the sofa where Jake was sitting.

"Thank you. I would like to propose a toast. To the beautiful, warm hearted and very sexy girl sitting next to me."

After I caught my breath, we tapped our glasses and the heat became unbearable. I looked in to his eyes and felt truly at home. It's the strangest thing. I've never felt this comfortable with anyone before. Not even when I first met Beth.

"I thank you for that but I must say you aren't too shabby yourself. You were so good with those kids today. You made us all feel at ease. "

"Before you say another word, I'm sorry but I have to do this."

He took both of his hands and held my face, he brought his lips to mine. Soft and gentle kisses. I pulled back at first, looked him in the eye and went back to his lips. He opened my mouth with his tongue and I let him in. His smooth, wet tongue was gently caressing my tongue and I felt like I was going to melt. He tasted of sweet wine, his mouth was hot and I never wanted this moment to end.

We both pulled away and then he pulled me into a hug. He was safe, comfortable and gentle. I really am in trouble with him. I never thought I believed in love at first sight, but I sure do now.

"Thank you for letting me kiss you Felicia. There's something about you. I wanted to do that since I laid eyes on you. Kind of strange in the situation we were in; my mind kept going to your beautiful lips."

Usually, I'm somewhat shy but I didn't feel that way with him. He makes me feel confident in myself.

"I have a confession to make. I saw you last week at the meeting about the Bishop kids and I haven't stopped thinking of you since. I know it sounds creepy, but something about you Jake is comforting. Your eyes are so kind and I'm so glad we were introduced today. It saved me from asking everyone about you. "

"I don't think it's creepy. I think it's cute. I saw you at the meeting but I didn't catch your name. I had heard your name after and was told about you. When I saw you today in Sandy's office I was excited like a little boy riding his bike for the first time without training wheels."

I was smiling from ear to ear. He took my hand in his and rubbed my palm. Damn, he is perfect.

"So how you do you know Dr. Sandy?"

"Sandy was my mother's best friend. My mom died three years ago."

Finding Home

"Jake, I'm so sorry."

"It was tough and it still is. It never should have happened. She died at the hands of my father. He was a drunk. He beat her; I tried to stop him so many times when I was young, nevertheless, he didn't, than he would beat me among other things. My mother finally got the courage up to leave him. She would have rather been dead than continue to be beaten. She was the sweetest woman. She didn't deserve that. They were high school sweethearts. Go figure. When she left, she didn't tell anyone where she was going. Not even me, but she kept in contact. He found her; lord knows how and killed her."

"I don't know what to say. Your mother would be very proud of you today. She didn't deserve that, nobody does. I'm sorry that you had to go through that too. I have to ask, is that why you went into Social Services?"

"Yes, I wanted to try and help others who had been abused. I was a police officer first and after seeing so many kids being hurt by the hands that brought them into the world, I knew this was where I needed to be. So, I became a Social Worker Investigator so I could play a part in bringing these kids justice and putting the sick bastards away."

"These kids are lucky to have you in their corner that's for sure. I feel the same way. I want to help other kids as well not go through what I went through. My mom died when I was seven of cancer and I was left with my drunken ass father. I would be lucky if I had bread to eat. He didn't care about me after my mom died; he took to the bottle and hard. So I was put into the system. He would leave me home alone while he was at the bar. When he was home, he was belligerent. He would throw things at me and curse at me, call me names and raise his hand. This was when he was drunk, if he was sober, which was rare after mom died, he ignored me. He said he couldn't take it because I looked like my mother."

I can't believe I'm opening up to him. The only people I have ever told was Beth and David and of course some kids at my earlier schools knew but not by me telling them. It feels like I have known him my whole life. It is the strangest thing.

"I was in six foster homes before I left. Let's just say, by the time I was nine years old I could have taken better care of myself than some of these foster parents. They were all in it for the money and could care less about the kids. As soon as I was old enough I left."

"Well, aren't we just a great pair. Felicia, I'm so glad we met. I feel like I've known you forever. I don't talk about my past with anyone, but with you it feels comfortable. It feels different to me. I don't know if it's because I see how caring and compassionate you are or that you have just shared things with me. I never just blurted out what I have been through with therapists."

"Thank you. I think I have been looking for that for a

long time. You are amazing."

"This is so weird to me. I, too feel like I've known you forever. I'm not usually proud to share my dysfunctional life but with you it's easy. I know I have been looking for you for a long time."

He took a hold of my head and brought me back to his mouth. We kissed and soon enough, we were lying down kissing. He caressed my head and I lay in his arms. This is where I belong, in his arms. This is right. We fell asleep on the couch. I haven't slept that good in three years. We both woke up to the alarm clock. He looked at me and said, "I'm so sorry. I never meant to stay the night."

"Jake, it was perfect. I'm glad you stayed. Yesterday was exhausting and I think today will be more of the same. I haven't slept that good in years."

"Felicia, I didn't mean to upset you with all of my baggage. I want you to know, I'm nothing like my father. I would never hurt a woman or anyone for that matter."

"Jake please, I shared some things too. Believe me; I have an airport full of baggage. Your eyes are too kind to hurt anyone and I can see that. I know we don't even really know each other, but you can tell me anything and I will never judge you."

He kissed the tip of my nose and gave me a hug.

FELICIA AND BETH

After Jake and I exchanged our Good Mornings, he kissed me softly and left to get ready for work. I didn't even want to shower. I didn't want to let go of his clean, musky smell. That's a smell I could really get used to. Reality is I must shower because I'll be seeing him at work after meeting with Beth for coffee. She's going to flip out when I tell her.

Quickly showering to get to the Diner early so I could fill Beth in, I'm usually late. Again, as I leave the apartment everything is bright and full of promise. I can't believe I met Jake Brown and he spent the night. He feels like my soul mate, so incredibly strange of my feelings but there is something wonderful about him. It is so easy and comfortable with him. That may all change if we ever become intimate when he sees my scars. I can't let my mind wander and become paranoid. Beth is sitting at our favorite booth when I arrive. For cripes sakes, I'm early and she's already here, so in her mind I'm still late.

"Hey Bethy, I thought I was early."

"What's with the Bethy? You haven't called me that in years?"

Finding Home

"I don't know. It just felt right. I'm in a good mood."

"Felicia Westfield, what are you keeping from me? I haven't seen that beautiful smile in way too long."

"I can't keep it in. I met him! OH. MY. GOD. He is fantastic and he slept over last night!"

"Hold on girl. You met who and what the fuck are you talking about he slept over?

"Jake Brown, you dumbass!"

"Holy Shit Felicia! Back up! You just told me you were dying to meet him. How the heck did you meet him and then him sleep over? Did you sleep with him? I can't stand it, tell me everything!"

"Okay, just slow down! I didn't sleep with him in the way you're thinking. I had a serious situation come up at work and he had to come and get the report. I nearly lost my breath when he walked in the door. He came to ice cream with my young client and me. Than we had to go to a house and it ended up being a crime scene. He wanted to go somewhere and talk so I asked him to my place."

"And…."

"He followed me home and we had a glass of wine. We talked. I shared some of my past and he as well. It was comfortable; I didn't feel like he would judge me.

I don't understand it but it just felt right. Bethy, he kissed me! I've never felt anything so fucking amazing before in my life. Then we both fell asleep on the couch."

"Holy crap. Did he see anything?"

"No, we kissed and talked and I fell asleep in his arms and that's it. It was heaven."

"Are you going to see him again?"

"I'll see him today we're working on the case together."

"Is it the Bishop kids?"

"Yes, but it is much worse than we thought. After seeing and hearing what I did yesterday, I can't believe I let him come to my place and kiss me. On my way home I felt guilty because of what the kids went through and I was being selfish."

"Hold on girlfriend, there is nothing selfish about you wanting to be happy and I'm sure those kids want that for you too. This is awesome Felicia. You are radiating happiness. Girl, I'm so happy for you. You deserve this; it's been way too long."

"This is going to sound crazy but I think he's the one. We have so much in common so far, of course, it's the bad stuff, but nevertheless we have a connection."

Finding Home

"Was he a good kisser?"

"If you like perfect. His lips were like fresh churned butter, so soft and creamy like. He was gentle and sexy. I could have kissed him all night without anything else."

"So, are you going to have sex with him? You have to get those cob webs out!"

"I have no idea. Plus, once he sees my scars he may not want to."

"Felicia, those scars speak of who you are and what you have been through and how you survived. Don't look at them as the nightmare that gave them to you. Look at them and remember, you are a survivor."

"Yeah, I guess you're right but it's still a bit unnerving. He'll ask how I got them and that will be just bringing it up again and I just buried it, you know."

"If you really feel this guy is the one, it's only fair to share the good and the bad with him."

"I guess I'll see how things go and take it from there. Unfortunately now that I filled you in, I must run. We've got a difficult day ahead and a great day as I get to see him."

"Okay, call me if anything else happens. Oooh, I can't stand it! I wish I was a fly on the wall."

"You are so sick Bethy! Nevertheless, I love you.

Have a great day and I'll call you."

FELICIA

While driving to the office, I start thinking about what Beth said. Not that I should be proud of the scars but I should own them and let them be a reminder of how strong I am and that I truly am a survivor. She may be my crazy, dirty mouth friend, but she is very smart and I love her.

I hope the kids slept well last night. I didn't get a call so that should be good news. I hope Kayla is holding up okay. So unfair. Joey, what the hell happened there? It's going to be tough talking with him today. I think Jake should handle that. Man to boy. I think Joey will take to Jake very well. I'm sure Jake will make sure he thinks he's cool first, that guy thing.

There he is, dressed in jeans and a white button down shirt. He's already with the kids and he's juggling for them with fruit. The laughter I hear from the kids is palpable. What a beautiful sight to see. I stand in the doorway in awe of the scene in front of me. Then

Finding Home

Kayla sees me.

"Miss Felicia, you look so pretty today. Did you sleep well? You look different today."

"Thank you Kayla. I slept exceptionally well. I'm not sure how I look different. How do I look different Kayla?"

"You look happy. You're smiling and you don't smile much you know. You need to smile more. It makes you really pretty."

"Kayla, you're right and I think I'll be smiling more."

Jake looked my way and winked at me. At that moment, I think he saw the biggest scar of them all. The one on my heart. That may be the only one that can be totally erased if he is around.

"Hey Adam, Joey, how did you guys sleep?"

Adam says, "I did good Miss Felicia, I didn't even cry."

Joey says, "I slept awesome. I didn't wake up once. This morning Miss Erin made us pancakes. She burnt a couple but they were good."

"Guys, I am so happy you had a good night. You deserve it."

"Kayla, how about you? How did you sleep last

night?"

"I slept like a baby; I haven't slept like that ever."

"It sounds to me like it was a good night all around."

Jake piped up and said, "One of the best."

His eyes stuck to mine like glue. It was a precious moment, a moment that truly connected us. We both knew as well that things were about to get emotional. Before we got started talking with Kayla and Joey, I had to go to my office and look at the pictures that Joey drew. I had planned to look them over last night, but I was looking something else over.

"Kids, Mr. Jake and I have to go to my office and go over some work. You guys hang out in here and play."

Jake left them the fruit to try juggling with. They were excited to try. He followed me to my office. As I closed the door so the kids wouldn't hear us, he grabbed me and kissed me with passion. He took my breath away.

"Sorry Miss Felicia, I had to do that. You are so beautiful! Just like Kayla said."

"No more! I won't be able to concentrate and we have to go through these drawings. But later I'd like more."

I gave him a huge smile and he showed me his fingers crossed. We each took two papers and began looking at them to see if there was some kind of expression in them. I began looking at one and my heart nearly stopped.

There was a drawing of a little boy with big teardrops falling on a bed. In the corner of the paper, there was a bigger stick figure with a lot of hair with a big smile on his face.

Jake had one with a stick figure lying down on a bed on its stomach with a paddle. A wooden paddle. The same stick figure man smiling and this one had a woman figure with long hair. The next ones we looked at was a flower and it said, "For Miss Erin." The next one were three stick figures holding hands side by side by size and flames surrounding them.

"Jake, what do you think these mean?"

"I think at the very least Joey was being beaten by the paddle. This is hard but I'm going to make sure he knows that he's safe now. I think we don't prolong it anymore and I'm going to take him to play catch at the park. I want him to think I'm cool, so he'll trust me."

"You're very cool, Mr. Brown. Let me give you some gummy bears to give to him. He loves them, especially the red ones. Okay, let's go get them."

"Hey Joey, Mr. Jake wants to take you to play catch with him, how does that sound? And Adam, Miss Erin is going to stay with you for a bit because I need to talk to Kayla. I'll be right down the hall if you need me."

"I'm not very good at playing catch but I would like to learn. I don't have a glove though."

"Well, Joey than I guess we will have to fix that won't we."

"Really, Mr. Jake? You'll buy me a glove?"

"You bet I will. Let's go so we can be back for lunch, okay?"

"Yes Sir."

Joey and Jake left; Adam was lying on the beanbag watching cartoons with his blanket wrapped around his hand. He was content. Kayla was a bit nervous but she took my hand and came with me.

FELICIA & KAYLA

"Miss Felicia am I in trouble?"

"No way! We just need to talk a little more so we can make sure Papa Harold never hurts anyone again."

"I don't really want to talk about it, it's embarrassing."

"Kayla, it's just you and me and there is nothing to be embarrassed about. I may even share a secret I have with you, okay?"

"Okay."

"Kayla, I'm going to ask you some questions and some of them may make you feel uncomfortable but you need to tell me everything, okay honey."

She stared at the wall and hesitated for a bit. She looked frightened. Somehow, I have to reassure her this is not her fault and she isn't bad because this happened.

"Okay, but I'm scared."

"I know honey but you're helping other kids. You don't want what happened to you to happen to anyone else do you?"

She shook her head no.

"Kayla, did Papa Harold ever hit you?"

"No, but Mama Cindy did."

"What did Mama Cindy hit you with?"

"A big wooden thing."

"Why would she hit you?"

"She hit me and called me a liar. She hit me when I didn't want to go to bed with the lights off and when I would cry because I wanted to sleep in Joey's room. She told me I was a baby."

"When did she start hitting you?"

"Right before Papa Harold started to come into my room at night."

"How many times did Papa Harold come in your room at night?"

"I don't know. I don't want to talk about that. I hate when the lights are off."

"Honey, I know this is hard and you're doing great. Did Mama Cindy ever come in your room at night?"

"Yes, she came in the last time and watched him hurt me and said I was getting what I deserved."

I had to take a break. That fucking Bitch, sweet as pie— fucking holier than thou Bitch. She knew about this but why would she protect Daniel and say that Kayla was lying? Did they do this to him too?

"Okay Kayla… do you know if they ever hurt Joey or Adam?"

"I heard Joey crying at night. I think they used the wood on him too. I don't think they hurt Adam."

"Can you tell me a little about Daniel?"

"Daniel is awesome. He always tried to stick up for me

with Mama Cindy, she didn't like me. He would even read to Adam. He was funny. His dad, that's why he's living at the Monroe's, hurt him. Miss Felicia, why would your company have us live with people that hurt us?"

My heart is completely shattered now. Trying to swallow the boulder that's now in my throat.

"Kayla, we didn't know that they would hurt you. They didn't tell us the truth. I'm so sorry! I would never want anyone to hurt the three of you."

"Why can't we live with you?"

"Oh honey, I would love to have you all live with me but I have a tiny little apartment. Plus, I'm boring. You wouldn't like living with me."

"Yes I would. Can we?"

I had to change the subject this was breaking me. I would love to have all three of them live with me but there's no way we could all live in a studio apartment and I have to work.

"Kayla, I'm so proud of you. You are a hero in my eyes. You are the bravest girl. We're going to find you three a wonderful home to go to and I'll still be around anytime you need me. We'll still go to the park and go on the swings. I will always be here for you Kayla, never forget that."

"I love you Miss Felicia."

"I love you too Kayla. Let's go check on Adam. We're done for today."

"Miss Felicia, can you buy a bigger house?"

"Honey, I wish I could, I wish I could."

JOEY & JAKE

"Joey are you ready to play some catch? Go easy on me, I'm not that good."

"You're lying! I bet you had a dad that taught you how to play ball?"

"Joey, I wish that were true but my dad never played ball with me. I guess we're even. "

Joey was thrilled with his new glove. He said it was the best thing ever. He'd never had anything new; everything he had was from the Salvation Army or Good Will. It was heart breaking but I knew the feeling.

Joey and I played catch for a while, meanwhile building up trust. Then I told him we should take a break and chat for a bit.

"Joey, I need to ask you some questions. You're not in trouble, so don't worry about that. Man to man okay?"

"You're going to ask me about Papa Harold aren't you? He's a bad man. "

"Yes Joey. I need to ask you about Papa Harold. Did he ever hurt you?"

"Yes."

Joey put his head down and started making a sad face in the dirt.

"What did he do to you?"

"He hit me with a piece of wood until I cried."

"Why did he do that?"

"He said I was a bad kid and I needed to learn to do as Mama Cindy said."

"What did Mama Cindy want you to do?"

"I can't say Mr. Jake."

"Why? You can tell me anything. This is man to man Joey."

"They said if I told anyone I would never see Kayla or Adam again. I can't be away from them."

"That's never going to happen. Papa Harold is with the police and he can't hurt you anymore."

"What about Mama Cindy?"

"She can't hurt you anymore either, we'll make sure of it. So can you tell me what Mama Cindy wanted you to do?"

"She made me touch her in her hairy spot. She held my hand there and moved it around. And when I didn't want to do it, she called Papa Harold and he would hit my fanny with the wood."

"Did Mama Cindy ever touch you in your private parts?"

"Yes and so did Papa Harold."

"What did Papa Harold do to you?"

"He hurt me. Bad. He didn't care. He told me he had to show me he loved me. Mama Cindy told me if I didn't touch her I would have to go live with my mother who didn't want me."

As a man, I want to kill these people. How sick can people be? How the hell did they slip under the radar? How many other kids have they abused? I have to breathe this boy needs me.

"It's okay Joey, take it nice and slow and remember you can trust me. You know what trust is right?"

"Yeah. I think I trust you. When I was sleeping, Papa Harold came in my room. He woke me up and he was rubbing my bum. He put some slippery stuff between my cheeks. Then he hurt me with his pee pee. He wouldn't stop and I cried, so then he got up and hit me with the wood. I was bleeding and they didn't care."

"Was Mama Cindy in the room too?"

"Yes, after he hit me he got on top of Mama Cindy and she was moaning. I think he was hurting her too."

"Joey, thank you for sharing with me. I know it was hard. I would like to tell you a secret too. My daddy hurt me too but he can't hurt anyone anymore. If I had told someone, like you told me maybe he would have stopped."

"So Mr. Jake, I'm not in trouble?"

"No kiddo, you aren't in trouble. You're helping and you are a real man. I think we better get back to the office to have lunch with everyone, sound good?"

"Yeah. Do you think I'm a bad boy?"

"Quite the opposite Joey. I think you're awesome. And we're going to find a good family for the three of you."

"Can I live with you Mr. Jake?"

"Joey, I only have a one bedroom apartment. I don't have room. But we can hang out and play ball anytime."

"You promise?"

"I promise."

Driving back to the office I feel like I just ran a marathon. I'm completely wiped out. I saw myself in Joey… afraid, ashamed and worried to be in trouble. Praying I wouldn't get another beating. We have to find these kids a great home they deserve love and safety.

Back at the office, Kayla and Adam are hanging out. I have a few foster parents coming in to meet the kids. They've been thoroughly checked out and neither of them have had any negative reports in the past.

We're going to let the kids choose this time. They need to be comfortable. This will be a trial and as long as their happy, they will stay.

"Miss Felicia, look at my new glove. Isn't it cool? Mr.

Jake taught me how to catch. Did you know his daddy didn't play ball with him either? He's like me."

"Joey, that glove is awesome. No, I didn't know his daddy didn't play ball with him. I think you're right little man, you and Mr. Jake are alike, both brave and handsome. You must be hungry, we had pizza delivered."

"I'm starving!"

The five of us sat around the table in the office apartment and ate pizza. Little Adam had more on his face than in his mouth I think. Kayla had three pieces; it was great to see her eat. Joey told us about playing catch and he had a sparkle in his eyes. These kids must feel much better now that they don't have to keep secrets.

"Kids, after we eat we have some people coming in to meet you. They're all really nice and they would love to have you all come stay with them. You get to choose who you want to live with too."

Kayla spoke up and said, "I want to live with you Miss Felicia."

Joey said, "I want to live with you Mr. Jake."

Adam just kept playing with the cheese on his pizza.

"I know you do but right now Miss Felicia and I don't have enough room where we live. We will visit often and take you all out; we're always here for you."

"You kids will like these new people. Like Mr. Jake said, we'll visit often and take you out. You can always call us too if you need us."

After we dodged that conversation from going further, the first couple came in with their daughter. It was Jessica and Andy Harper and their daughter Lucy. Jessica was a nurse until she had Lucy and Andy is in banking. They seem lovely. They became foster parents after they found out they couldn't have any more children. They didn't want Lucy to be an only child. Lucy is ten years old like Kayla. I really think this is a good fit.

The kids fell instantly in love with them. They didn't want to meet anyone else. After they heard they have an in ground pool with a slide, they were sold. Jake and I watched them interact and we both felt at ease. Andy Harper talked baseball with Joey and that was a clincher. Adam was already hugging Jessica Harper.

We had Erin call the other families and cancel them. They were going to live at the Harper's home, which was conveniently only about two miles from my apartment. The Harper's had been briefed about what these children have been through and with Jessica's nursing background, she was ready for the challenge of possible nightmares and backlash.

While Jake and I were talking with the kids, all of their things were picked up from the Monroe's house and

Finding Home

Cindy Monroe was arrested. In a short few hours, things had taken a turn for the much better.

Jake and I followed the Harper's to their home to get the kids settled in. They seemed excited and Kayla and Lucy were fast friends. They lived in a four bedroom Colonial home with a decent size yard. It was in a neighborhood with lots of kids. The Monroe's house was in a secluded development and there weren't any kids, this will be great for them.

The kids picked out their bedrooms. Adam and Joey will share a room so Kayla could have her privacy. Being a ten-year-old girl that was important. Joey was happy and Adam was excited to share a room with his big brother. He said Joey would keep the monsters away.

We both gave them all great big hugs and let them get adjusted to their new home. The Harper's would be getting visits often from me and they were fine with that, even the unannounced visits, this gave me a trusting feeling.

Jake and I looked at each other and we both had a tear in our eyes. These kids are finally home. Jake and I did it together. He connected with Joey, and I with Kayla. Of course we both loved Adam, how could you not, he was a love bug and a half. We left the Harper's house and decided to go to the park ourselves. It felt fitting for what we had both experienced with Kayla and Joey there.

FELICIA & JAKE

The park was so beautiful, the trees and the bushes were carved out as animals. I love this place. It has special meaning to me and the Bishop kids and now, I'm sure Jake. There were mothers with their children and dad's playing ball with their sons. Happiness and sadness embraced Jake and I. We were silent for a bit. I think we were both taking inventory of what we never had as children but then to the possibilities that now surround the Bishop kids. So many emotions have bombarded not only the kids but Jake and I as well.

I still had the blanket from the picnic yesterday so I laid it out on the ground under the same tree that Kayla had confided in me. I asked Jake if he wanted to go on the swings and he said not right now.

"Felicia, can we just sit and talk? I want to know everything about you."

"Sure, but I'm not so sure you want to know. It's not all butterflies and roses."

"I know that feeling."

"What would you like to know Mr. Brown?"

"How come someone as kind and beautiful as you isn't taken?

I stared at the ground and made sketches in the sand. Just like the kids did. Completely nervous about my answer. He sees my hesitation and I clear my throat.

"I had a very bad relationship in college. I haven't been ready to meet anyone but that changed the day I saw you at that meeting."

"Really?"

"Yes. Now why is this gorgeous, gentle, sexy guy in front of me not taken?"

"I guess you could say I've been chasing demons if you will. Living in fear that I would turn into my father and I would never want to hurt a woman.

"Jake, you aren't capable of that. You aren't your father."

"I know I'm not. I hate that man and what he did to my mom and me. You just hear stories all the time you know and it's always been a fear of mine."

"Have you not had any girlfriends?"

"Yeah, I have but nobody like you. Nobody I could share who I really am with. I never told anyone what I already told you. Who would want a guy that his father killed his mother?"

"I would. You're a caring and compassionate man who seems to have taken all of his misfortunes and turned it into a way to make a difference in people's lives. Even though we just met, I know you're a good man and I trust you."

"This is so weird Felicia. Why does it feel like we've known each other forever? You hear about that in the movies but I never thought it happened in real life."

"Maybe it's our time to be happy. I think we both have had enough tragedies in our lives. Maybe it's fate."

"Fate… I like it and I like you."

He took my hand in his and kissed it. Then he kissed my mouth and my body was aching. It didn't matter there were kids running around, for this moment, it was he and I.

"Well, I like you too Jake."

"Felicia Westfield, will you go steady with me?"

We both cracked up laughing.

"I would love to go steady with you Jake Brown."

This is incredibly natural and easy with him. Maybe this really is fate. Is it possible to love this man so soon? Beth is going to freak out if I tell her that, although she'd probably be happy.

"Jake, do you think the kids will be happy with the Harpers?

"I think it was fate that we found them on the list. I think I really can get used to fate."

"I agree with you. As much sadness that we saw today with those kids, I think they are now where they belong."

"I think we all are."

He kissed me again and this time, it was undeniable that he wanted more. It scares me and excites me at the same time. I want that too but I'm afraid he will find me disgusting.

"Jake, this is really bothering me. Will Kayla and Joey have to testify in court? I don't ever want them to see the Monroe's again."

"I'm going to try for them not to. I'm hoping our statements will be enough. If not, I would like Kayla and Joey to tell their stories again being recorded. It won't be easy for them to say it again but it will keep them from testifying. Once the DNA comes back from Kayla's exam that may be all we need."

"I hope so; we still have to meet with Daniel as well. This is long from over. There may be many more victims."

"Sadly, I think you're right. We should probably head back to the office and finish the paperwork for the transfer. Then we can stop for the day. I would love to cook you dinner, if you would say yes."

"You cook? I'll have to see this. I would love to. Let's hurry up and get through that paperwork. You'll have to let me cook for you if you cook for me tonight."

"You got a deal."

We folded up the blanket and walked hand and hand back to the car. We both were quiet on the ride back, both processing the day's events and this newfound relationship. I'm happy for the first time in way too long. This gorgeous, incredibly delicious man next to me is a gift sent from someone or something. I'm accepting it and my past and with the help from each other, I think we'll both move forward from here.

We worked fast and diligent completing the paper work to make Kayla, Joey and Adam's transfer official. It's a bittersweet moment that it had to take such repulsive abuse for these kids to find a good home. I hope their scars will heal, in time at their pace.

As I stared down at my signature on the transfer papers, from behind me, I felt a slight breeze behind my ear. Jake was here and ready to go.

Finding Home

"Jake, can I go home and shower first?"

"You can shower at my place."

"That's sweet of you but I think I'd like to shower at home and change my clothes, if that's okay."

"Sure, why don't you bring a change of clothes along? Tomorrow's Saturday and you might want a fresh pair of clothes for the morning."

"Really? Are you inviting me for a sleepover Mr. Brown?"

"It's only fair. I slept at your place last night."

He gave me a grin that made me want to yell, "Take Me Now!"

"I'm not that kind of girl ya know."

I laughed and he followed.

He gave me his address and I went home to take a shower, but I had to call Beth first. I think I need a pep talk.

"Hey Beth, What's up?"

"Hey Girlfriend, not much, just trying on my new thong. Jim's taking me out to dinner for a surprise and I want to give him something afterward. If you know what I mean?

"Yeah, yeah, I know what you mean Beth. Have fun with that. Listen, I'm going to Jake's place for dinner, he's cooking. I had to come home and call you first because, well, you know, I'm a chicken."

"Felicia, everything is a risk in life. As I have told you a million times before, if you don't take them, you will always wonder what could have been. What are you afraid of? From what you've told me he is an awesome guy?"

"He is. I'm afraid I already love him. That's fucked up, right?"

"Felicia Westfield, you said the F-bomb. I'm so proud of you. You must be serious if you are using that word. Hey, stranger things have happened. I think what you two have already shared together in this incredibly short time is more than most shares in a lifetime. Go with how you feel and never be ashamed. You deserve to love and be loved."

"I think it's my time Bethy. I think I could go all the way with this guy."

"You have to go for it. You so need to get laid."

"I didn't mean it that way; I meant I could spend the

rest of my life with him. And I think I could go all the way that way too."

We both chuckled. My stomach was literally somersaulting and my mind was dancing around the remote possibility. I feel so alive. The only way I used to feel alive, like my heart still beat was when I relived my torture from David. This, this is alive in the way of living; every sense of mine is heightened. I'm alive and loving it.

"As you always tell me, if it feels right do it. You are in complete control. Hey, Jim just got here. I have to get dressed so he doesn't see his surprise for later. Follow your heart and let loose girlfriend, you don't know what you're missing. Call me tomorrow with the dirty details."

"Sometimes, I really wish I was like you Bethy. I'll call you and good luck with the surprise. I can't wait to hear what it is."

I think Beth is right; I have to loosen up and not question everything. The past is the past it's over. The more I think of it, I really do want to feel that again. If his kiss is any indication of what is to come, than holy shit! It's been so long since I had an orgasm not by my own hand. My lower region is throbbing. I better get in the shower and make it a cold one.

Jake

I can't believe how nervous I am. Felicia will be arriving shortly and I can't seem to wait a minute longer to hold her in my arms. This is messed up for sure. I feel like I already love her. It's been forty-eight hours it can't be real. I think of her and I can feel my heart pounding, in a good way, not the fear kind I am used to. What if she sees my scars?

With every fiber of my being, I want to make love to her. I want to feel, see and taste every part of her body. If she sees my scars she could be really freaked out. I'm fearful of that. The scars are there and they represent who I am. We didn't have the money to have them skin graphed. I wish we had.

I want her so bad it hurts. I want her to know and trust that I will never hurt her. She is the one for me. I don't know how this happened but I think it really is fate. Three days ago, I was sullen and lonely. Living my life for the system, trying to hide my pain by helping to bring justice to the kids. In addition, put the fucking bastards that scarred these kids as I have been away. Now, my life has made a complete turn. The future looks and feels good to me for the first time in my life. I know with Felicia, I want to share all of myself with her. And her to me. I like this.

I had better get to cooking or she'll think I'm a phony, promising to cook for her. Shrimp Scampi over angel hair pasta. A wedge salad with Bleu Cheese and French bread. I don't even want to eat dinner. I just want to kiss her, touch her, and hold her. My jeans are getting tighter at the mere thought of her. How can this be happening? There she is, ringing the doorbell. I opened the door for her and before me was the most beautiful girl I've ever laid eyes upon. Her hair was down, straight and long. She had a hint of light pink eye shadow on. Her cheeks were blushing, not sure from make up or being nervous. Her lips, oh her lips glistening with a clear lip gloss. She was wearing a pink tank top under a see through white blouse, tied loosely and jeans. She was petit and smoking hot.

"Are you going to let me in or are you just going to stare at me?"

"Oh sorry. You look magnificent Felicia."

"Why thank you but you don't have to say that. I'm already staying the night, we have a sleepover planned."

Shit, my jeans are getting tight again and the zipper may just burst. Must deflect.

"Are you hungry?

"Starving! It smells delicious."

"I hope you like Shrimp. I made Shrimp Scampi."

"Get out, that's my favorite meal, did you talk to Erin?"

"No, it's my favorite too."

FELICIA

I want to just wrap my arms around him and kiss him until I can't breathe anymore. It's as if he's in my soul.

"A glass of wine for my Steady."

"Thank you!"

We sat down at his small round table in the kitchen; he had the lights dimmed and Michael Buble playing in the background. He fed me my first bite. It. Was. To. Die. For. I then fed him a bite, reached over and kissed him. This was another moment I'll never forget. Two souls becoming one.

We laughed and didn't talk shop at all. We talked about the most bizarre things, almost avoiding any heavy conversation. I told him about Beth and Jim and how Beth is a bit on the wild side. He told me about his friend Bubba from the Police Academy. It was light and comfortable.

After dinner I helped him clean up and then we went and sat in the living room. It wasn't big but it was cozy. At least his bed wasn't in the same room as the refrigerator. He put on James Taylor and he pulled me off the couch in his arms to dance. How did I have my prayers answered? His mouth devoured mine with heat and ownership. He released my swollen lips and kissed over my ear and whispered something in my ear, that I wasn't sure I heard right. No, it couldn't have been. It was getting hotter by the second and I could feel him getting hard against me. I pulled back, to catch my breath, walked away from him and went in the bathroom. I splashed water on my face to wash the tears of pure fear and disbelief off.

"Felicia, I'm sorry. Did I do something wrong? Please come out. Let's talk. Nothing else."

"I can't Jake. I want you too much."

"C'mon Steady, come out. Please talk to me."

I opened the door a crack and he had his eye in the crack looking at my one eye peeking through with a lone tear falling. He pushed the door slowly, took me by the hand, and sat me on the sofa.

"Jake, I'm so sorry. I'm embarrassed; I made a fool of myself by hiding in the bathroom."

"No Felicia, don't think that. I know this is happening so fast. I was beyond nervous before you got here, I get it."

"Jake, there's something you don't know about me. I don't look like other girls. I have scars."

"Felicia, I have scars too. Do you want to talk about it?"

"No. Yes. I'm afraid you'll think I'm ugly and

disgusting. This is the first time in three years I have been with a man. I'd be lying if I said I was not fucking terrified. I don't swear much, sorry."

"It's okay. I would never think you are ugly and disgusting. Are you kidding me? You are the most beautiful woman I have ever seen, inside and out."

"Jake, kiss me please because it may be the last time after you hear what I have to tell you."

"I'll gladly kiss you but it definitely will not be the last time, no matter what."

"Okay, here goes. When I was in college, I had a boyfriend. His name was David. We went out for a couple years. He started drinking and changed. He hit me and told me I was nothing special to look at and no guy would ever want me. I broke it off with him. He kidnapped me a few days later."

I am really crying now. The only people I ever told were Beth, my therapist, the police and Dr. Sandy. The words coming out of my mouth, I can't believe I'm telling him this so soon. He held my hand tighter and told me to take my time.

"This is hard Jake. I never thought I would have to tell a man this that I cared about because I never thought I would allow myself to care again."

"You're doing great, Felicia. It really is okay. I want to know the good and the bad about you."

Finding Home

"David blindfolded me and brought me to some cabin in the woods. After we got there, I pleaded with him to take the blindfold off. I felt that if I could look into his eyes, I could make him stop. He then gagged me with the blindfold, tied my arms to the bed and my legs. I was helpless Jake. I couldn't stop him. He had a gun and knife. He raped me. I was raped."

Hysterically crying, somehow telling Jake made it feel like it just happened.

"That son of a bitch, come here, let me hold you and make you feel safe. You're safe with me, I promise."

"I believe you. That's not all though. After he raped me, he put the knife inside me, then the gun. I thought he was going to shoot me up there. He was enjoying himself. He told me no guy would ever want to be with me when he was finished. He was going to be the last guy to ever fuck me. He took the knife and grazed my neck with it. Then he started kissing my breast and saying horrible things. He then carved his name across my chest. He beat me until I was unconscious. He drugged me for days so I stayed asleep. I have scars Jake, they aren't pretty."

"Was Dr. Sandy your doctor?"

"Yes. Why?"

"She told me about you, not your name of course. She was devastated; she never saw anything like it. She told me how unbelievably brave you were. She didn't think you were going to survive. She said that girl, which I know now to be you, changed her life."

"Did she tell you everything?"

"I don't know?

"Did she tell you I can't have kids?"

"She had said the girl had to have a hysterectomy. I'm so sorry Felicia. You didn't deserve that. You're still beautiful to me, I promise."

"After I saw you at the meeting Jake, without even meeting you, I saw your eyes, the kindness and safety they designated. That was the moment I knew I had to move forward. If I had never met you, you would still be the one person that changed me and made me see color again and hear the sounds of nature and traffic and you made me see myself as pretty for the first time in three years and for that, I'm forever grateful."

"Felicia, that's the nicest thing anyone has ever said to me. I have to tell you, that you have made me come alive. Just three days ago, I was miserable, lonely and sad, actually feeling disassociated. I'm so grateful for you and I really believe we met each other by some higher power. This isn't a coincidence. It can't be."

"The scars won't turn you away from me?

"Felicia, I have something to show you."

He lifted up his shirt and there were scars all over his chest —many round ones. He turned around to his back and more of the same. I was still attracted to him; he was still beautiful underneath the scars.

"Jake I'm so sorry, but they don't bother me other than the fact you got them from pain being inflicted upon you. They are who you are and what Beth tells me it shows that we are survivors. We are survivors Jake. I truly believe even more now that we were brought together for a higher good. Maybe it's our mother's up in heaven getting us together."

"I guess Beth is a smart lady as you said. I never looked at them like that. I only saw pain and remembrance of how my mother didn't survive his hands. I still feel the cigarettes burning my skin Felicia. Every day when I see them they are a reminder. Beth is right; I'm a survivor and these scars don't have to hurt me anymore. Maybe you're right; our mother's may have sent us to each other. That's a really cool thought. Felicia, there's something I have to tell you but I'm afraid its ridiculously early because there's still so much to learn about each other."

"What is it Jake?"

"Felicia Westfield, I think I'm falling in love with you."

A smile surrounded my face and my heart surely skipped a beat. He feels the same as I do, I can't believe this is happening.

"Jake Brown, I think I'm falling in love with you too. I've never felt the way I do with you. Even my first boy crush. I know this isn't just newness. I have never felt that I had a home since my mom died and the last two days, I have felt at home. Is that crazy? I feel like this is all crazy."

"Up until now, I honestly never believed in this kind of thing but now that I'm living it, I know it to be true. You are my destiny."

"You do know Jake that people will have a lot to say about this fast-paced love affair."

"Felicia, as early as I can remember, I've always wanted to be loved and to give love. I've loved two people in my life, my mother and my Nana and my other grandparents I never knew. As I grew older I was afraid to love because the two people in the world I ever had were gone. My grandmother died a terrible death from lung disease. As far as people having something to say, they haven't experienced what we have. What matters most to me is that we found each other."

"Jake, I am so sorry. I don't care what anyone thinks either. You're right, what matters is that we found each other and we know it's real."

Finding Home

Forty-eight intense hours. Jake knows everything there
is to know about me. My sucky childhood, my drunk
ass father, David and there's really not a lot more to
know about me, except seeing the scars in physical
form.

"Felicia, we can take this as slow as you want. I won't
touch you or look unless you approve. I want you to
feel comfortable and at ease with me. I'll never judge
you Steady."

"Jake, I think I'm ready for you to see me, all of me. I
have to say, I like the nickname."

It began and the desire was undeniable. The need was
intense. We needed each other; we needed to heal
these scars inside and out. Jake took my hand in his
and led me to his bedroom. I looked around, it was
plain, no headboard on the bed which was a great start
for me. The walls were painted a pale blue and
there were no pictures on the wall. A bureau and a
nightstand, that's it. Ironically, I found it to be soft and
crisp.

We stood staring in each other's eyes and I knew it was
all okay. I knew that I wanted him to make love to
me. This wasn't about sex; it was about connecting as
one. He was causing an inferno between my thighs

and tachycardia.

I lifted his shirt over his head and began caressing his scars, one my one. I kissed each one and although his body quivered he didn't stop me. His abs were solid and still beautiful despite the permanent markings and these markings speak of who he is.

He spoke to me in a soft raspy voice, "Now it's my turn. I want to see your beautiful body."

A lump developed in my throat but I didn't stop him. He pulled my shirt over my head and left my lacy bra on. Jake gave a new definition to sexy and compassionate. His mouth was working magic down my neck and slowly, he slipped his finger under my bra strap and pulled it down. The letters were no longer visible after the skin grafts but the scars were now upfront and personal to him. He massaged over one breast and dropped a tear from his eye. He lowered the other strap and then took the entire bra off. I was fully exposed to him, showing him my biggest insecurity. He kissed my nipples gently and with tenderness, I felt all of the sensations.

"Felicia, you are undeniably the most beautiful woman I've ever seen. Your body is flawless to me."

I couldn't stop the tears from falling. They were tears of happiness for once in my life. Nobody besides Beth has ever said I was beautiful before. I love this man.

"Don't cry Steady. If you want me to stop please tell

me."

"I don't want you to stop. Make love to me."

He was hard and ready. I wanted to touch him everywhere. I held him in my hands and he took my jeans off. He was so damn hot and sexy. He looked into my eyes and I knew we were one. The connection was explosive, in a good way.

"Are you okay Felicia?"

"I'm better than okay Jake, don't stop."
"Can I touch you there?"

"Yes, please."

With his large gentle hands, he began to lightly rub my sensitive spot. All the while holding my hand with his other hand. He was sympathetic to my fears. Between my thighs was blazing, so close to the edge. My legs began to shake and I became breathless. The intensity was spectacular. I couldn't hold on anymore. He was taking me over the edge to ecstasy.

"Steady, you are so wet. Do you still want more? I want to make love to you, slowly and gently."

"I want you to make love to me like I've never wanted anything before."

He brought his soft and oh so supple lips to mine. His tongue was exploring mine and he placed himself inside of me slowly. I gave out a moan and he knew it was pleasure and not pain. My hands on his incredible ass and I pulled him in further. My hips matching his every move. He never took his eyes from mine. He began gasping for air and I could feel him throbbing inside. He put his hands through my hair and made love to my mouth as he released inside of me.

We both lay there, unspeaking but knowing. Knowing we both found home. Then I saw his mouth start to move, but no words were forming.

"Thank you Jake."

"Felicia, the thought of anyone hurting you makes me feel things I never want to feel. I'm so angry and enraged at what that guy did to you. To hurt such an amazing woman. I'm sorry you had to experience that. Nobody will ever hurt you again. You are a hero in my eyes. I will keep you safe forever and longer."

"Jake, I feel the same way about you. The thought of anyone hurting you makes me want to retaliate. But from this point forward, we have found each other and our demons are getting weaker and soon enough they will die away."

"Felicia, I never thought I would ever feel love again. I never thought I would have a home but with you I have both things that I thought were impossible."

"Jake, do we share the same mind? What you say is what I'm thinking. Do you believe in soul mates?"

"I believe in everything good now. I have never made love to a woman. It's clear to me now that it was always empty; it's never been like that. I've never taken my shirt off with a woman. I wouldn't allow it. I was ashamed. I've never in my whole life felt so safe. I've never had forever in my mind but because of you and what you just gave me I can now look forward to it Felicia."

"I never thought I would ever feel love along with pleasure again. In fact, I know I have never felt anything like I did making love to you. You have given me life back. A life I only dreamt of but you're real and you're my moving forward, Jake Brown."

Still naked in his bed, as comfortable and secure more than I ever have been. His fingers are giving me chills up my arm as he lightly touches. His eyes are a bright blue with a green halo, simply stunning. The gentleness of this man beside me is pure and honest.

"Hey Steady?"

"That's not fair; I don't have a nickname for you."

"I'm sure you'll figure one out soon. I want you to know something. I want you to know I will never fuck you. I will only make love to you tonight and always."

"Stop making me cry Bright Eyes. I got one. You are so darn sweet. I'd ask you where you've been hiding all my life but I think I know. This is meant to be. I feel it in every part of my body and mind. It was timing."

I was so afraid I would feel pain if a man went inside me after the attack. I never could have come close to imagining that it would feel amazing. I couldn't be happier to have waited for Jake. He's nearly my first in a way.

In just several hours, I know I don't want to be without this wonderful scarred man. I hate that he was given the scars but I'm okay with them. They show me all of him. They don't make him less beautiful, they make him more.

"Felicia, I have a question for you? Have you ever thought about looking for your father?"

"Jeese, that's a mood changer. Yes and No. I think about it and I get scared, scared that he wouldn't want to see me. Frightened that he would hurt me. But then I think maybe he's changed and maybe he's clean and sober now and he would love me. Then reality sets in."

"I still have connections at the Police Station if you're ever interested. I want you to have what you want, always."

"Jake, it's something to think about but I'm not ready yet. I just found happiness and I don't want any gloom clouding that. How about you? Have you ever gone to see your father in prison?"

He shook his head now and looked down at the floor.

"When and if you're ever ready, let me know. I'll be by your side all the way."

"I think someone would get hurt if I went to see him and the last thing I want to do is share a cell with him."

"I don't blame you but maybe it would help you if you saw him and told him how he hurt you and what it did to you. Also, it would be nice for him to know that he didn't win. If he was such a cruel man, possibly hurting you was his way of feeling in control. Maybe you should go to him and tell him he no longer has control over you. I'll go with you."

"How about we put these two bastards out of our mind for a while and enjoy each other. I'd much rather feel your body and make you feel good."

"I can't argue with that Bright Eyes."

Such depth in our conversation and I think it was getting to Jake. At this moment, I think he wants to feel good and not have lingering thoughts of the tragedy and turmoil he went through.

Our mouths are close as we stare in each other's eyes as if we are breathing the same breath. He lowers his mouth to mine and it starts out soft and picks up pace to desperation of need. I need him just as much.

He is touching every part of my body. Electrical

currents are shooting through my body.

"Felicia, just lay back and let me make you feel things you haven't felt before. Let me love you, touch you, smell you and taste you. I need you to feel everything. I want to make you feel as beautiful as I think you are."

Tears begin again. I do as I'm told and lay back and watch him softly kiss and touch my body in a way I've never known. I can feel every nerve ending being affected. I feel everything and more intensely this time. The fear isn't there and I'm letting loose as Beth would want me to. Here and now, it's just him and I. No scars, no past, just love, trust, and want.

"Jake, you're making me crazy."

"In a good way, I hope?"

"The best way."

"Let yourself go Felicia. Feel it in your soul. This is love and pleasure."

"I can't hold on anymore, Jake. Oh Jake, Oh Jake!"

"You are so incredibly sexy Steady."

"Make love to me Bright Eyes; I want to see those eyes glow."

With that, he entered me tenderly. We adapted to each

other instantaneously. His hips and my hips moved in conjunction creating a tidal wave of sensations. His eyes are surely glowing as he put his mouth on mine and succumbs to the pleasure. Jake and I are one, there's no other way to describe it. We both were breathing heavy but satisfied beyond words. At least I am, from the sounds he was making, he is too.

He lies on his side, stroking my hair and I began to fall asleep. This is the best sleepover ever.

The smell of maple syrup and bacon is waking me up. I feel next to me and it's empty. Jake is cooking again. I gave my body a huge stretch, grabbed one of his t-shirts from his dresser, and went to the kitchen.

"Good Morning Steady! How'd you sleep?"

"Let me think…..peacefully."

"Are you hungry? I have pomegranate juice, pancakes and bacon."

"Famished, it sounds and smells fantastic."

"Come on over and grab your plate. I got an idea in the middle of the night; I wanted to see if you were up for it."

"Okay, what are you thinking about in that gorgeous mind of yours?"

"I was thinking, this may be weird, but, I was thinking that we both hate our scars, right?"

"Go on."

"I thought today we could change them by getting tattoos."

"Are you kidding? They would have to do my whole stomach and yours and your back to cover them all. That will hurt like hell and I'm not sure if you know this, but I'm a chicken. "

"There's no way you're a chicken. You're full of it. You are the bravest person, man or woman that I know. What do you think?"

"I don't know, maybe. What would we get?"

"For you, Steady, I was thinking about an Angel, because that's what you are to me. Maybe you can pick something out for me."

"I kind of like that Bright Eyes. I'll have to think about what fits you best. Are you sure you'd want to do that? What about if we aren't together? Do you want to have something so permanent?"

"Yes, I want something that permanent. I love you Felicia Westfield and I want both of us to get rid of our scars so we can build our life together with just great things ahead."

"Let's do it! You really are an amazing man Jake Brown. Brilliant too, I may add."

"Then it's settled. We can take a shower and then head on over to the tattoo parlor. There's a good one that the cops go to that I know are sanitary. They have books we can look through and we can find the perfect fit for each other."

"I'm excited now. Let's hope I stay this way and don't chicken out when I get there."

"Don't you worry; this pain we may feel will go away quickly, it won't last a lifetime. It's time to let our pain lose its power."

FELICIA

He kissed me and walked me to the bathroom to shower. He always seems to know the right things to say. Beth is going to be so proud of me for letting loose. I'd say getting a tattoo is letting loose.

As I get in the shower, my eyes focus on the remnants of my attack. These scars have been a part of me for way too long. He's right; it's time to cover them with something that gives us good memories. Turning the old scars to a faded memory. Everything's moving so quickly. I find myself pinching my bare skin with the water trickling over me to see if this is real. Turning the heat up and then to cold, I feel the jerk in my body when it gets cold, this is real, it's not a dream.

After my shower, Jake took one.

JAKE

Running my hands over the indents of permanency over my stomach, I wonder… would a tattoo erase the pain or only mask it? I just can't see the circles everyday anymore. I can't see the scars. They're eating me alive. It has to be done; it's a step in the right direction for me and for both of us. It will be like a new beginning together.

Her body is beautiful even with the scars but for her as well, it's a brutal reminder. A miracle has come to me, never did I think possible. Felicia is that miracle. We flew into each other like a tornado, but as I think about it under the beating water of the shower, it isn't the amount of time we have known each other; it's the connection, the content and the souls we have shared. I'm ready to start anew and cover these scars.

FELICIA

When Jake got out of the shower, he had an intriguing look in his eye.

"Hey Bright Eyes. Are you okay?"

"Yeah, I was just thinking if getting the tattoo is just like a band aid for the hurt or if it would be more than that, like a new beginning for us?"

"I had the same thought and I decided I really want to do it. For me, it will make me think of you. It will make me think of possibilities, love, freedom from fear and safety."

"I love the way you think Felicia, you're right, let's do this!"

We walked into Expressions Tattoo Parlor and my heart began to palpitate. There was a teenager having a tattoo put on his arm and I saw the needles. I was never a fan of the needles, just like Kayla. My mind began to wander to the Bishop kids. How were they doing?

Jake got my attention and showed me a book that I could look at to pick his tattoo. Right away, I found it. A Maple Leaf. It says:

"In China and Japan the Maple Leaf is an emblem of lovers. North American settlers used to place the Maple leaves at the foot of their beds to ward off demons and encourage sexual pleasure as well as peaceful sleep."

This is perfect for him.

"Look at this Jake, its perfect."

"Felicia, I love it! I found this for you. Angel wings with a halo in the middle. What do you think?"

"I love them but I'd like them in a light pink."

"They'll do any color you want and it'll be beautiful, just like you."

Jake is only going to put the Maple Leafs on his front and not the back. One-step at a time. Each angel wing will be on each of my breasts and to me it will symbolize healing and love.

Jake and I were called back to the room where we would be inked up in. They would have two different artists doing them. I will have a female and he, a male. There's a curtain between us so the man won't see me. Thankfully I can talk with Jake through the curtain if I need to.

After all the colors were chosen, they began. When the first needle went in, I felt nothing. No pain. As she continued, I still felt no pain. Of course, I felt something but nothing in comparison to what gave me the scars.

Jake was quiet on his side of the curtain, with an occasional squirm, but he seemed to be doing well. I guess this is where mind over matter came in. We both wanted a fresh start and this to us is what would help erase so many reminders. That's probably why the pain wasn't bad.

Finding Home

They ended up doing both breasts today, which they didn't think they would have time. Apparently, colors make a big difference in how long it takes and I only had one color. It had taken six hours, which was much longer than I had thought. I have absolutely no clue about tattoos.

They opened the curtain when we were both finished and gave us a minute to see each other. I looked at Jake and his eyes jumped out even more to me with the green leaf on his stomach. It was beautiful. Even more so that I know what it means. He looked at me and a tear left his Bright Eyes.

This is art for sure; I have a new respect for the tattoo parlor. This takes skill and talent. They told Jake and I about the after care and warned us that it will be very sensitive for a while. Certain materials will feel better than others will.

"I didn't think you could be more beautiful, but I was wrong. I'm speechless; Felicia and I don't get that way often."

"Jake, I didn't think you could get more beautiful either, I love it and I'm not speechless. I can't wait to run my hands over that leaf and kiss it until it has dew on it."

We were both happy with the body art we now owned. The scars will never go away in our minds but on our bodies, there will be less. This was the right choice.

After we left the tattoo parlor, we went back to his place. It was exhausting getting them done, so we took a nap after lunch. I woke up to my cell phone ringing. It was Beth. I told her I would call her back but she insisted she meet Jake and asked if we would go to dinner with her and Jim tonight. I asked Jake and he said sure.

FELICIA & BETH

I had to go home and get some clothes for tonight. We were going to go to an Italian Restaurant. On my way home, I called Beth and asked her to meet me at my place; I had something to show her. She had no idea what it was, but she was on her way, knowing her she'll beat me there and I'll be late again.
Sure enough, as I pull in the parking lot, she's waiting for me.

"Jeese Bethy, were you already at my house when I called?"

We both laughed.

"You got me all curious. Felicia what is it? I can't stand it."

"Hold your horses! Let's get inside."

"Hurry up and open the damn door."

We went inside and I unbuttoned my shirt, no bra on, a bit sore.

"Holy shit Felicia, it's gorgeous. Damn you have nice boobs, not too big, not too small."

"Stop checking me out, you pig. Do you really think the tattoo is good?"

"Yes, but what the hell possessed you to do that? You are the biggest chicken I know."

"Jake."

"Is he kinky or what?"

"No, it's not like that. Sit down; I have lots to tell you. Jake has scars. I have scars. His father beat him and his father murdered his mother. He thought that if we covered the scars we could move forward and let the old scars fade away. I was scared at first but the more I thought about it, the more I liked the idea."

"Wow, his father killed his mother? What the fuck Felicia. There are some sick ass people in this world. I think it's great, he sounds pretty smart to me. What did he get?"

"A Maple Leaf. They are said to get rid of demons and enhance sexual pleasure."

"That's awesome. So, did you have sex with him?"

"Bethy, I can feel again. Oh god, can I feel again. Leg shaking orgasms, you were right, I had to loosen up.

He was incredible with me, to me and in me."

"Holy shit girl, you got laid. I'm so happy for you."

"Beth, I have never felt this way in my life. He's so gentle, compassionate and fucking sexy."

"There you go again using the F bomb! I am loving it."

"I have a question for you though Beth. Is it really possible to love him after 48 hours? He has seen inside my soul. It's like we are one, it's so weird and amazing and scary and amazing."

"Felicia, I don't think there's a time limit on when you fall in love. I think it's rare in my opinion, but that means to me that if you feel it, you have to grab it while it's there. I believe in love at first sight, first sex, and first kiss and all of the above."

"I love you Bethy girl. So, what was Jim's surprise?"

"He took me to this Japanese Restaurant where we had our own private, tiny room. We ate on the floor with chopsticks and he fed me. He is now the Assistant District Attorney."

"That's fantastic Beth. Are you happy?"

"Similar to you, blissfully. His salary will jump up dramatically and he wants to buy a house for me."

"That sounds like you are moving forward. I'm so

happy for you. Plus, he'll now be putting the bad guys away. Oh, did he like your thong?"

"Let's just say he may as well have used it as dental floss."

We laughed, we always laugh together. She's a no holds bar kind of girl.

"I'm excited to meet this famous Jake Brown. We'll have a great time tonight, it'll be good for Jim to go out and have some fun. He has a week off before he starts the new job, so we'll be house hunting. Tonight is a celebration of you, Felicia, I can't say enough how happy I am that you are finally happy. I never thought I would see you like this."

She actually had a tear come down. Beth doesn't cry. She's strong like a bull. We gently hugged and she left to get ready, as did I.

What a day today, hell what a last three days. I saw three kids being affected by abuse. I'd be lying if it didn't bring back memories. Memories I hate owning. Meeting my soul mate, making true love for the first time and changing the look of my scars by the tattoos.

JAKE

Soon I'll be meeting Felicia's best friend. So much so fast and I'm just in a trance over how awesome it feels to have something in my life other than pain.

When the needle went in the first time during the inking, I wish I could say it didn't bring me back to the past. I can't seem to shake the image of my mother at the stove cooking dinner, humming and feeling happy. Me by her side helping her, or more like getting in her way. Just the two of us. Then he walked in the door, the humming stopped and her protective mode went into place. Mom was immediately transformed to a baby bird with a broken wing.

Dad came in the kitchen and saw that mom was cooking chicken and he hated chicken. That was it.

"You know I hate chicken, what the fuck am I supposed to eat," dad raised his voice.

"I'm sorry Ed, I just thought you would like this, it's a new recipe," my mom shyly said.

"You never think of me do you bitch? You only think of yourself and that fucking son of yours," dad said with his voice reaching a higher octave.

"Ed, he's your son too and I do think of you. I just thought that you would try it again and see if you liked it. Plus it was on sale and you know money is tight," mom pleaded.

My dad took the fork from her that she was using to cook and scraped it along her arms. He then slammed her face into the sizzling pan of chicken. I just watched for a minute, frozen in time. I then took a step forward and he came at me.

Finding Home

"You little fucker, mommy's little boy. Do you want some too," dad came at me with the fork.

"No daddy, please no!" I begged and trying hard not to show my fear.

He pushed me to the ground. All I could hear was mom saying, "Ed! No! Stop! He didn't do anything!"

Then the sobs. I tried not to cry because crying made the beating ten times worse. He took the fork that he just labeled my mom with and ran it down my stomach. He pressed down hard to insure he left his mark and there was blood. I hated blood. He left me lying on the floor and stormed out of the house.

Mom made sure he was gone for sure and then helped me up and wiped all the blood from me. She had burn marks on her face from the hot skillet and her arms were a bright red with lines from the fork. I was ten years old but when he raged, I felt like I was only two.

Mom and I would always locked ourselves in her bedroom after he worked us over and she would hold me and rock me back and forth. She never let me go until I said so. She was selfless, she was my mother and I miss her.

Remembering those tumultuous days, my whole body trembles. The guilt I carry everyday that I didn't stop him. I couldn't stop him. I look down at my chest and those marks are soon to be invisible. I feel a sense of calm come over me. I haven't had a nightmare in three nights and that's a blessing. Felicia doesn't know about the nightmares. The thrashing and the blood curdling screams. I hope being with her will make them never reappear.

With her, I think healing has begun. She's going to be here any minute. I better snap out of this pity party. No sooner did the doorbell ring she was here and I miraculously feel better knowing she's behind that door wanting to see me and love me.

Opening the door was what I think Christmas morning should have felt like. There was the biggest gift staring back at me. The gift of love, hope, forever and beauty.

"Hey Bright Eyes, how are you?"

"Much better now that you're here."

Jake was wearing a pair of cream pleated pants with a navy blue, soft cotton button down shirt. His eyes were crystal clear blue, like the Caribbean Ocean. His eyes went green or blue depending on what he was wearing. He was luscious in every sense of the word. I, had a pink sweater on and a white skirt and we complemented each other well. If you haven't noticed yet, pink is my favorite color. It was my mom's too. We both had to choose soft fabrics because of our new ink; I wish I could go bare-chested. I'm sure Jake feels the same.

Jake pulled me to him and took a deep breath, and kissed me with such force, I lost my breath, literally lost my breath. It was amazing, but something was behind it.

"Felicia I love you. Promise me you'll never leave me."

"Jake, what's wrong, I'm with you forever, I'll never leave."

"I'm okay, just this feeling when I am with you; it's really like home. Now I get what you said about being home. I want home; I want you to be my home."

"What are you suggesting, Jake?"

"Let's just say, I know this is crazy and like a whirlwind, but I want to come home to you every day. I want to hear your heartbeat close to mine at night. I want to keep you safe. I want to wake up to that beautiful smile of yours every day. I want you to move in with me, Felicia."

"Like a permanent sleep over? There are things you still don't know about me. I have nightmares, although I haven't had any since I have slept next to you. I would love to move in with you, I want the same as you. Going to bed and waking up to those eyes, will make me safe, feel loved and that's what I want, so the answer is yes Jake."

"How about if we look for a new place. One that is truly yours and mine?"

"That sounds fun. Are you sure about this Jake?"

"Never more sure about anything Steady."

"How's the Maple Leaf feeling?"

"Tender, but in comparison, not bad at all. How about you?"

"When they were putting the needle in, I kept thinking that I've endured real pain, pain that was meant to hurt me. This was a pain that was to help heal, so I didn't think of the pain. Honestly, right now, I feel like my left boob is simmering in hot coals and my right one is smoldering."

"I wish I could make them feel better Felicia, but I think I'll refrain."

"I think that's a good idea for a bit Jake, thanks. Not that I don't like you touching them, but I think I'd just rather you admire them from afar."

We both started laughing and realized time was passing by.

"We'd better get going to meet Beth and Jim, she's really going to give me crap for being late, which I always am anyway."

The restaurant is a small and quaint place. Dimly lit and the aromas of Italian are enticing to the appetite. There they are, Beth and Jim, sitting at a booth with a red and white checkered tablecloth. Beth waved us over.

"Hi Beth, hi Jim, this is Jake Brown, "I introduced them.

"So nice to meet you both, Felicia's filled me in about you both," Jake said with a hint of nervousness.

"Nice to meet you too Jake, she's told me all about you," Beth said with a devilish smirk.

Beth looked at me with a wink and thumbs up, down low. Jim got up and shook Jake's hand. This is a good start. We talked about everything from Jim's new job and their looking for a house. Jim and Jake hit it off, they talked crime and punishment and Beth and I sat and listened to their conversation and were both in awe how much we loved these men.

We ate our dinner and laughed so much my stomach hurt. It was a natural and not forced night with Jake, he had no issues with showing attention to me or jumping in on any conversation.

Jake decided to announce to Beth and Jim that we

were moving in together. I thought Beth would spit up her drink, you know the kind when it goes up your nose.

"When did this come about Felicia? You didn't tell me this," Beth questioned, thinking Felicia was holing out on her.

"It just did, about five minutes before we left to meet you," I told her.

"Jim, what do you think of this fast and furious relationship? My best friend is finally come out of her cocoon," Beth asked.

"Well, stranger things have happened. You would never know by looking at them they just recently met, I say go for it, love is precious and when you find it, you have to grab hold of it," Jim responded.

Jim kissed Beth on the mouth, in front of us and something in me told me that things were going to be moving right along for them as well.

"Hello guys, you're talking like Jake and I aren't in the room," I said with a giggle.

"Sorry girl, I think I speak for both Jim and I, we're both thrilled for you! Happiness is written all over both of your faces. Jake, welcome to our world," Beth said looking at both of us with sincerity.

"Thanks Beth. Believe me, I know it's crazy soon, but

Finding Home

I can honestly say, Felicia is my soul mate and I love her with all of my heart. I will keep her safe and protected and that is a promise," Jake spoke and grabbed my hand.

This suddenly became a tad uncomfortable to me, but it's Beth and she likes all the information upfront. Jim kept staring at Beth then he spoke.

"Jake, I know what you mean man, when Beth and I met, that was it for me. She keeps me on my toes and alive. She makes me want to be better and encourages success, when some women are intimidated by it. She is my soul mate as well. I believe in that stuff, but not until I met Beth."

"Jim, I love you that was so sweet. We better get out of here; I just want to wrap my arms around you," Beth said while pulling Jim from the table.

"Bethy, don't hold back now. You two go ahead, we'll head out in a minute. Thanks for meeting us tonight, it was awesome. Call me tomorrow," I said with a wink.

"Jake, I think I have to thank you for coming into Felicia's life, I think Beth will stop worrying now. Give me a call and we'll play some racquetball," Jim said while shaking Jake's hand.

"Jim, it's my pleasure. I'll give you a call; we have a tedious week at work, so I may have to burn off some steam. Good night Beth, pleasure was all mine," Jake said and gave Beth a hug.

What a fantastic night. The man I love, my best friend, and her love. Everyone just clicked and everything feels right in the world. Jake and I left the restaurant, hand in hand and we went to my place. Seems as though we take turns at each other's place, but I'll be saying good-bye to mine, so I wanted to go there.

"Felicia, you have some great friends. Beth is a riot, she says it like it is and I like it. Jim, he is great, I think we'll get along just fine. But, you, my Steady, you are the best of them all."

"You're too sweet Jake. I know they loved you too."

On the way home, Jake went into the store and picked up a newspaper to look for apartments. He wasn't wasting any time. When we got to my place, I changed my clothes into sweats and a t-shirt. When I came out of the bathroom, Jake was sitting on the couch with no shirt on. His tattoo was breathtaking.

"Bright Eyes, you are Hot! Not sure if I can focus on the tiny letters in the newspaper with your masculinity stares at me."

"What did you have in mind," Jake questioned with a raise of his eyebrow.

"I'd prefer to show you," I responded with a whisper.

I wanted so much to rub my hands on his chest, but

the maple leaf, I'm sure felt more like foliage. I told him to lay back and let me pleasure him. What's fair is fair. I kissed his lips and joined my tongue with his to give my mouth the moisture I needed to do what I want desperately to do to him.

He was erect and ready for me. I started at his neck and went down to his happy trail. Then I did it, I took him in my mouth and looked straight in his eyes as he bucked his hips and released himself. I want nothing left to the imagination with him. To please him is to open my wings.

"Wow, Felicia. You are amazing, once again. I want to see you and feel you."

I took it upon myself to take my shirt off and let him see my Angel Wings; it had little peeks sticking out now. I really felt free and secure with my body, more than I had in the last three years.

Jake lightly kissed my inked breasts, he was afraid they would be tender. So he went to other areas on my body.

"Jake that feels so good. You feel good."

"Felicia, these are the two most beautiful, delectable breasts I've ever seen. Keep telling me what you like and I will do it to make you feel like you make me feel."

"Jake, I don't want you to stop touching me. Your

hands are magical and you make me tingle in all the right places."

He touched every orifice of my body, with every touch; I shivered and became more and more weakened by his touch. He watched as I climaxed and he was again ready himself. I wanted this to be his time to enjoy; I got on top of him and rocked back and forth on him, feeling him deep inside me. His tattoo was my focus because his eyes shadowed it. He is an incredible lover.

Exhausted, shaky and oh so satisfied, I couldn't move, I didn't want to move. He got up and grabbed the newspaper. We lay in bed flipping through the apartment guide and circled the ones that sounded good. We fell asleep shortly after our lovemaking.

Monday morning, oh how I hate Monday's. Jake got up before me, of course, made coffee, and left me a note. He had to go to his place and get ready for work.

To My Steady Angel:

You looked as pure as your wings sleeping. I didn't want to wake you. Forgive me for just leaving. I want to thank you for being you and coming into my life. I know things are moving so fast and I couldn't be happier. I truthfully have never felt so at ease with anyone. You have given my life a second chance and I want to do the same for you. I can't wait for us to live together and build on the incredible thing we have already. I love you Felicia Westfield to the moon and back!

See you at work,

Jake

A girl could get used to waking up to a letter like this. The added perk of having my coffee ready and waiting for me. Today I'm not meeting Beth at the Diner. It feels weird but things are changing with both of us for sure. She's going to see houses today, so we're going to have our morning coffee on the phone together.

Dialing her number, I'm anxious to hear what she has to say about Jake. The phone is ringing and ringing and that is very odd she knew I'd be calling. I left her a message hoping she'll call back before I head into the office and face the reality of this investigation.

She never called back and I had to get to the office. Jake and I were meeting with the police today in regards to the Bishop kids and with Daniel. We need to find out if he's a victim too. I'm so glad that Jake and I had the weekend that we did because I see us being emotionally exhausted as the week goes on.

Jake poked his head into my office.

"Good morning Miss Westfield. How are you this

morning?"

"I'm perfect, how are you Mr. Brown?"

"Happy and in love."

"Really... do tell?"

We had to shut my office door because there were eyes everywhere out there.

"There's this girl that I recently met, she has the most gorgeous smile, infectious laugh and a smoking hot body. She's an angel from heaven."

"That's funny because I'm in love too. This guy has hypnotizing eyes that reach into my very soul. He makes me laugh, he makes me so insatiable and his body is of perfection. He is my angel from heaven too."

Then he cupped my cheeks in his hand and planted a sensual kiss on my lips. My head is spinning and my body is mush from his touch. Not so sure how this working together thing will work.

"It sounds like we both found who we were meant to be with Felicia."

"Without a doubt."

We smiled and knew that this had to stop; we had to get serious and think of the Bishop kids. We drove to the police station together and Jake was briefing me on how this will all work. We're both hoping that we can figure out a way these kids won't have to go to court and see those monsters.

We're meeting with Captain Patrick Murphy. Jake was a police officer with him before he became captain. It's so weird for me to walk into a police station, I haven't had to do this since I was seven years old and that was frightening when they took me in the squad car and put me in a tiny room until Social Services could get me. They wanted to keep me safe but I felt like I was in trouble. Jake must have noticed the apprehension I had walking through the doors. One foot was not in front of the other.

"Hey Felicia, are you okay? You seem scared. Your face just got pale," Jake said to me behind concerned eyes.

"Let's just say, being here brings back memories. I'll be fine."

I can't help but think of my mom's frail body lying in that hospital bed. Nearing death, she couldn't speak or do anything. My dad was holding her hand, crying, and begging her not to leave him. He had such kindness in him before mom passed. I sat there and watched the love of his life pass away before him. The mom that gave me life and love every day she was alive. Then it all changed. Months after she passed, I was sitting in this same police station, alone, confused and abandoned because my dad couldn't love me anymore because I reminded him too much of my mother.

The metal door opened and Captain Murphy came out.

"Hey Jake, thanks for coming down. How've you been? We all miss you around here," said Captain Murphy while shaking Jake's hand.

"Patrick, it's good to see you. I think I have a better chance of helping these kids doing what I'm doing now, but I miss you guys too. This is Felicia Westfield, she is the Bishop kid's Social Worker."

"Nice to meet you Miss Westfield," the Captain extended his hand.

"Same to you, Captain Murphy."

"Shall we get started? Would you two like something to drink," the Captain offered.

We both declined. We followed him down the long bland hallway to the interrogation room. Everything will be recorded, which is good, but we're not being interrogated.

"Hey Cap, we have to figure out a way that these kids don't have to testify. They've been through too much already and it was hard enough for them to talk."

"Jake, we don't like to have kids testify either, but the

problem is, Harold Monroe has a reputation in town and he's worth millions. He isn't going to just accept these charges and I'm sure he has the best attorney money can buy."

"Captain Murphy, excuse me for saying so, but I don't care how much money he has, he's a pedophile and he doesn't deserve even a trial as far as I'm concerned."

"Miss Westfield, I agree with you, if all of these allegations are true, he is one sick and twisted bastard. The reality is, money talks and if his attorney wants those kids to testify and create doubt and dismantle their credibility, he will fight to no end to get it."

"Cap, can we video the kids and their statements? This will be agony enough for them, they just were placed in a great home and I think they both want to forget. Little do they know, they will never forget."

"Has the DNA come back yet from Kayla's rape kit?"

"No, we should have it by the end of the week."

"Captain, once that comes back and if it proves that Harold Monroe raped Kayla isn't that enough? Why hasn't there been anything in the newspaper or on the news about the Monroe's arrests? Is that because of money too?

"If and that is a big IF his DNA matches the rape kit, than we are less likely to have to have the kids in the courtroom, he'll probably plead out. As far as no news on these two, you got it, money can buy silence too."

"Cap, it seems as though you are protecting the two of them. Can I ask why? With the information we gave and the evidence found at the house, this should be an open and shut case. Please don't tell me, you're falling for the money too?"

"Jake, let's just say Harold Monroe has given this community and our station an outpouring of support monetarily. I'm walking on thin ice. I have to make sure everything is 100% or the Mayor will be up my ass. Cindy Monroe was very convincing, I must say, but the good thing is, they're still in custody until the arraignment which will be the day after we get the DNA."

"Cap, I think we're done here, please let me know as soon as you get the DNA results back. I can't say that I'm leaving here today feeling like you are on the kid's side, sorry to say."

"I have a question for you Captain Murphy. Have you ever been abused, sexually or otherwise? Have you ever lived in foster care and were treated like you were a no good loser," I blurted out with a trembling voice.

"No, Miss Westfield, I can't say that I have."

"I'm happy for you, because there is no greater pain and for you to sit behind that Captain's Uniform and even suggest that these people will get off because of money, you haven't met me yet. Good day to you."

Wow, I can't believe I said that to him. That son of a bitch is no better in my eyes than Harold and Cindy Monroe. Jake turned to me, put his hand on my lower back and led me out of the room and down the hallway to the exit.

We didn't say a word until we got in the car. I began to sob at the sickening thought of those kids not getting justice. Jake held me and told me, we will not stop until those kids get justice.

"Felicia, I didn't know you were so feisty. I was so proud of you in there. Patrick Murphy has obviously turned from good cop to bad cop. I could see it in his gestures and his eyes. If this is so, I will take him down too."

"Jake, I want the media to know about the Monroes. I have a woman at the paper that owes me a favor; I'm calling her and giving her a story. These kids deserve a voice and maybe more kids will come forward."

"Felicia, this could get messy but I'm with you if you're up for the backlash."

"He's guilty as sin, he won't have any backlash. He deserves to be exposed and if there are other kids out there that have been abused by them, I want them to feel like they can come forward. I could give a rat's ass about those sick fucking pigs."

"Okay, okay, we'll do it. After we meet with Daniel,

we'll go to the paper."

JAKE

I think I just fell more in love with her. She stood up to the Police Captain, she was brazen and to the point. She is fighting for what's right and there is no way I can deny her that or myself for that matter. We work for the kids, we are their voice, and they will be heard.

The rest of the ride from the Police Station to Daniel's respite home was silent. My pulse feels like it's out of control. I have to calm down before we get there. I'll be no good at finding anything out if I'm a wreck. I pulled the car over before we reached their street.

"What are your doing Jake?"

"I think my angel needs a hug."

He put the car in park and pulled me into an embrace that made me feel safe.

"Felicia, we will do whatever we can within our power to put these sickos away and give these kids what they so deserve….justice. Let's take some deep breaths before we get to Daniel. This could be another ugly story or a dead end; we have to prepare for either."

"I can do this Jake, I promise, I won't let you down or the kids down."

"I have no doubt. Let me give you one more kiss before we go."

"I love you Jake. You really know how to make me feel better."

He put the car back in drive and he took the left onto the street. A cute neighborhood, the houses weren't big but they were maintained. He pulled into the driveway and squeezed my hand to let me know, it will be okay. Neither Jake nor I have met this foster parent, Nicole Anthony and Geremy Anthony. They are a younger couple.

Jake rang the doorbell and Nicole came to the door.

"You must be Mr. Brown and Miss Westfield, come on in. Don't mind the dog. She loves people. Daniel has been waiting for you," Nicole welcomed us in.

"Thank you Mrs. Anthony, it's a pleasure to meet you," I said with a smile.

"Daniel, they're here, come on in the kitchen okay," Nicole motioning for Jake and I to follow.

"Hi Miss Felicia. I didn't do it," Daniel said with conviction.

"Daniel, we didn't say you did honey. This is Mr. Brown, he's an investigator for Social Services."

"Hey Daniel, please call me Jake."

"Hi Jake."

"Daniel, Jake's going to talk with you for a bit, you're not in trouble, so please don't be afraid. I'm going to talk to Nicole. I'll come in and talk with you in a bit, okay?"

"I know this isn't fun, I'm sure you would much rather be doing something other than talking to me, but it has to be done. Remember what Miss Felicia said, you are not in trouble. Why don't we go in the den and talk," Jake says while trying to make Daniel feel comfortable with him.

"Okay," Daniel agreed.

The two of them left to the den. It was a small room with a door so they could have privacy. Mr. Anthony isn't here yet, but he's on his way. I'm going to talk to Nicole for a bit to see what she thinks.

FELICIA & NICOLE

"So Nicole, how have things been going with Daniel since he's been here?"

"He's a good kid. Down to earth but pained as well. He is quiet most of the time and he loves the dog. He's been taking her for walks and the dog has really taken to him."

"Dogs are great for healing. Nicole, has he told you

anything at all about his foster parents?"

"He told me he didn't ever touch Kayla. I have to say, I believe him. The other night we woke up to him screaming in his bedroom, he was having a nightmare. I went and sat on his bed and rubbed his back and he got really scared. Still quite groggy from his dream, he blurted out, don't touch me, please, no more, I didn't do anything wrong."

Tears welled up in Nicole's eyes. What a sweet woman who very obviously cared about children.

"Did he say anything else afterward?"

"No, he fell back asleep."

"The next day, did you or he mention the nightmare?"

"I did. He didn't want to talk about it. My husband took him out for a drive and he talked to him, but he promised Daniel he wouldn't tell me what he told him because he's ashamed."

"I see. Will your husband be here soon?"

"Yes, he had a meeting that he couldn't get out of; he should be here very soon."

I can't help but wonder how things are going in the den. Jake is so good with kids, if Daniel has been abused in anyway, Jake will find out.

JAKE & DANIEL

"Daniel, I'm going to ask you a few questions but I want you to know something about me first. I want you to know you can trust me and if there is anything I understand, it's being abused. I understand your father abused you. Sucks huh? Me too. My dad's in prison for killing my mom. I'm going to turn on the recorder now. This is just in case we need it in court."

"Okay. Wow! Jake I'm sorry about that. So you really were abused?"

"Yeah, I hate that it's true but in every sense of the word I was abused. How long had you lived with the Monroe's before the Bishop kids came?"

"A few months."

"Were there any other kids living there when you were there before them?"

"Yeah, there was Rachel, I think thirteen and Johnny was eleven. They were really quiet. They didn't talk to me much."

"Okay, so how was Mama Cindy to you?"

"Friendly."

"What do you mean by friendly, Daniel?"

He lowered his head and I could tell this was the moment of truth.

"She treated me differently than Rachel and Johnny. She was nice to me."

"Was she not nice to the other two?"

"No. She was mean and would call them losers and that no wonder they were not loved by their parents."

I find my fists clenching and heat radiating to my face. Anger was surging.

"What else can you tell me about Mama Cindy?"

"Jake, they will kill me if I tell."

"They can't hurt you anymore Daniel. I promise."

"Promise?"

"I sure do."

"Mama Cindy would come in my room when I was asleep. She touched me. She made me touch her. Fuck. I tried to say no and Papa Harold would come over with the paddle if I didn't touch her. She told me I was her special one."

"Man, I'm so sorry. You're doing great. Did Papa Harold touches you?"

145

"This is so fucking embarrassing. You'll think I liked it."

"No I won't. Please just tell me what he did to you. If he hurt you, you'll be helping other kids too. You seem like a great guy. I'm sure you don't want this to happen to anyone else, right?"

"Jake, it never goes away. I feel dirty and different. How can anyone ever love me after what they did?"

"Daniel believe me, you will be loved. I never thought I would be either but I am and I love again. Take a deep breath and keep going."

"Papa Harold came into my room; I wasn't sleeping when he came in. He had crazy eyes. He sat down on my bed and told me that I was the most special kid they have ever had. He told me he loved me. Mama Cindy came in the room too. She had the paddle in her hand. I knew something bad was about to happen. He told me he had to see if I was a real man. He pulled down my shorts and boxers and began to stroke me. I kept saying to stop but he wouldn't. He was hard and he was enjoying it. Mama Cindy started to kiss me and then she told Papa Harold I was ready. He jammed his penis in my mouth. I couldn't breathe. I tried to move but she had me held down. He kept pushing my head back and forth, he was choking me and he came in my mouth. I threw up on him after."

What the fuck? This keeps getting worse and worse.

"Daniel, I know that was hard. This wasn't your fault. They are sick people. Is there any other time they came in your room?"

"Yes. This time I was asleep. Papa Harold came in and put some slippery stuff on my ass and he put it in. I was in a dead sleep and I was lying on my stomach. I couldn't stop him. It hurt so badly. It felt like my insides were coming out with every thrust. I'll never forget it, the pain, the violation and the fear. I didn't want it."

"Daniel, I know bud. I know— can you go on?"

"When I started to cry, Mama Cindy got the paddle out and hit me in the back with it. He got out of me and they went on the floor and had sex. That's it. They ruined me."

"Daniel, it seems like that now— I know. Believe me, I know. However, as long as you know that you're safe and that these are some mentally ill, sick people and if you don't give them power you will recover. It takes time, lots of time but you will heal. I promise. I honestly don't think it ever goes away completely but it gets better once you are in a healthy environment and believe that it wasn't your fault."

"So you don't think I'm disgusting or that I wanted it or enjoyed it?"

"Absolutely not! I think you are a brave man. I think your honesty here speaks to how much you care about others. So, how did you get along with Kayla?"

"Kayla was awesome. We were friends. I tried to protect her, Joey and Adam. I guess I failed at that."

"No, you see that you couldn't stop them from doing what they did to you. How could you ever have stopped them from doing it to them? This is not your fault. Promise me you'll stop blaming yourself."

"Can't promise that. If I would have told someone they wouldn't have been hurt. I don't think I will ever erase the memory and the pain that man caused me. He took everything away from me."

"Daniel, you did what any kids would have done. You obeyed to save your life. That's all you could have done. They were the horrible ones not you. These people made you think that this was okay and it was out of love. As a child, a defenseless child at that, your choices were taken away."

"So what happens now Mr. Brown?"

"We'll need to go to the police. The good thing is we recorded your statement so you won't have to relive it."

"Am I going to be taken from here?"

"Do you like it here?"

"Yes. I feel like I belong. I really like Nicole, Geremy

and the dog."

"We'll see what we can do about you staying here.
Daniel, the very sad truth is there are sick people in
this world and you were the victim. It's always easy to
blame ourselves and think we could have stopped it
but in reality, we were trying to stay alive. There is no
excuse for human beings like them, they deserve the
highest punishment and we are going to do everything
within our power to get you all justice. "

FELICIA & THE ANTHONY'S

Geremy Anthony finally got home. He told me what
Daniel had told him. It was tough for him to get the
words out of his mouth at times. He was sickened by
it. They really enjoy having Daniel in their home and
they would like to keep him permanently.

"Mr. and Mrs. Anthony, I would approve him staying
with you but you need to know with this kind of abuse
there is aftermath. He will probably continue to have
nightmares and could become depressed if he isn't
already. It won't be all roses. Let's not forget you'll
have the teenage hormones."

"Miss Westfield, Geremy and I have discussed this in
length and this is the reason we became foster parents,
to change a child's life. We know these kids come
from a place where things weren't easy for them. We

want to give him a home, a real home."

I found myself reaching across my chair to hug Nicole. She is genuine and loving and I think Daniel will progress well in this environment.

"I think Daniel is lucky to have you two. I'll draw up the paperwork and transfer it over to permanent placement. I can't stress enough how Daniel needs love and trust and needs to believe that this wasn't his fault."

"We will get him all the help he needs. He will be loved here, Miss Westfield," Nicole said with a tear in her eye.

Jake and Daniel came out of the den. Jake gave me a look of pure sadness. Daniel seemed to be more relaxed.

"Hey Daniel, I want to tell you how brave you are and that you are safe here with the Anthony's. I have no doubt about it. How would you like to stay here," I asked.

"Miss Felicia, really, can I?"

"I'm going to fill out the permanent placement paperwork. You will be staying here."

"Thank you. Wait... do you two want me here?"

"Daniel, we want you to be here. The dog wants you

to be here. We're going to arrange for some counseling and we'll all work on this together. This is your home. Your home Daniel," Nicole stated.

Daniel went and hugged both Mr. and Mrs. Anthony and he had tears rolling down his face. Another bittersweet ending. A kid has to be victimized to get to where he belongs. Jake looks completely spent. This isn't an easy job but the rewards are priceless.

Jake and I left the Anthony's home silent. The looks we exchanged were knowing and no words needed to be said. He drove back to the office. I happily filled out the forms for the change in Daniel's placement to permanent. My stomach was growling but the thought of eating made me sick after the day so far.

Jake was on the phone with the police reporting yet another victim. He was to drop the tape off without me later. I picked up the phone and dialed my connection at the Telegram, Amanda Styles. I told her I had a big story for her and I needed to speak with her in person. She told me to come right down to her office. I knew if I didn't eat something I would pass out so I quickly ate a yogurt and pushed through the urge to vomit.

This day has taken its toll on me. Money or no

money, status or no status, the Monroes will pay for what they did to these children. I told Jake I would talk with him after he went to the police station and I went to the Telegram.

On my way over to the Telegram I tried to call Beth's cell again. Still no answer. This is weird. I left her another message. Something is off here. She has to call me back and soon.

I sat down with Amanda in her office and started by telling her that this is a very sensitive story. There will be no kid's names used. She agreed. Amanda was stunned by what she was hearing. She knew Harold Monroe as everyone did. He had big bucks. I found her being hesitant.

"Amanda, please don't tell me you have funding by him as well?"

"Harold Monroe is by boss's cousin. Felicia, I honestly don't care. I'll risk my job to help put these sick people away. You have my full attention."

"Thank you. I'm glad to see you're one of the good ones. This has to be like an anonymous tip. That would probably protect us both from your boss."

I continued and told her everything. The story would run in tomorrow's paper, front and center. It just so happens that her boss was on vacation so it made it easier for her to get the story out there.

Jake was at the police station hopefully having an impact on them and their previous protection of the Monroes. I never had money so I never knew what money could buy. Apparently it can buy people and freedom and that is despicable.

JAKE

"Cap, I think what I have here will make you change your mind about Harold and Cindy Monroe. Hit play and you'll see," Jake's voice was gruff and forceful.

We both sat and listened to the tape. It was appalling to sit and look at Captain Murphy and see his wheels turning. He muttered many Hmm's. To hear Daniel's voice so broken and shattered made me sick and I had to vomit in the barrel. It was impossible to not think back to when my own father, my flesh and blood made me do the same thing Harold made Daniel do to him. He held my head down and wouldn't let me come up for air. I threw up again.

"Jake, are you okay?"

"No Cap… I'm not! To think you would protect this son of a bitch for money, I've lost all respect for you. You are an officer to protect and serve! Not to be bought!"

"Jake, it runs a lot deeper than that. My family is at risk. This man has power and lots of it."

"You're a fucking cop for Christ Sakes; you have all

the means you need to protect your family."

"He's not just a one man deal. If he's behind bars it doesn't end there. This family is brutal if anything jeopardizes their millions. !hey will go to extremes to prevent it and I mean extremes. He has cousins that are involved in his protection and they are paid dearly for it. He's threatened my family."

"It looks like the child molestation is just one of the many sick things he has up his sleeve. I'll tell you what, I don't give a shit! These people need to be off the street and I won't sleep until they are. We're done here; I'll take the tape with me. Good Luck to you Cap."

JAKE & JIM

That son of a bitch! I don't buy it for one minute. He's being paid to mess up evidence and such. Harold Monroe inherited his money, probably invested and gave back to the community for notoriety. I'm not buying that there's anything else. Maybe he threatened Captain Murphy that he'll be shut off financially if he doesn't mess up this case.

It's time I get the big guns involved. Jim doesn't start at the District Attorney's office until next week but maybe he could do some side work. I'm calling him. This is too much for this Police Department to handle or mishandle.

Dialing the phone, it's ringing and on the third ring, he

answered.

"Hey Jim, its Jake Brown."

"Hey Jake, what's going on? Did you hear the news?"

"What news?"

"Oh sorry. From the sounds of it you haven't heard. Is Felicia with you?"

"No she isn't. What's going on Jim?"

"David is being paroled."

"Doesn't he have another two and half years to serve?"

"Of his sentence yes, but his daddy is a big time Boston attorney with lots of connections. It takes a bit of time to finalize it all, so there's still some time before he gets out. He has to go through the stages and if he is acceptable afterward, he will be released to the community."

"Honestly Jim, I'm not sure I can handle another fucking psycho getting away with their actions because of money and who they know."

"It appears he has gone through Alcoholics Anonymous Program and hasn't been ticketed for fights while incarcerated. The way that system is if he behaves and is a good little boy they'll consider parole.

I'm sure his father is guiding him through and making sure he doesn't fuck up. Sorry Jake. What did you want to talk to me about?

"I need your help. Now that you'll be the Assistant District Attorney, I need you to help me keep some people behind bars."

"Who are we talking about?"

"Harold and Cindy Monroe."

"Oh shit Jake! What's going on there?"

"They've been sexually abusing their foster kids; they are sick, fucking excuses for human beings. They are both in custody until the DNA comes back."

"Why has this not been on the news? Jesus, this is headline news. This guy is huge around here. He helps out so many causes."

"His generosity is a cover up for his perverted mind. So far, we know of three kids he and his wife have raped and beat. We're at the very beginning of the investigation. Been down to the station to go over things with Captain Patrick Murphy but he seems to be conspiring with Harold Monroe. There's something big here Jim. This really smells."

"So, why have we not heard about this in the media?"

"They're being paid off to keep it quiet and to mess up

evidence."

"Now that I think about it, Patrick Murphy's house was just up for foreclosure. I think he went to Foxwoods one too many times. It's funny because it is out of foreclosure already. You're right Jake, this is smelly."

"Can you help me? Can you help these kids?"

"I'm going to call the office and let them know I'm starting tomorrow. This can't wait a week. Jake I'll let you know what's going on with David too. I wouldn't say anything to Felicia about it; it may end up being a mute point. Maybe he'll screw up, let's hope. We'll get these kids justice and find out what smells at the Police Station. Glad you called Jake."

"Jim, I'll do anything I can to help. Oh and Felicia is at the Telegram right now giving them the story."

"Holy Shit! Harold's cousin owns the paper. This could be bad. You both need to be vigilant; I don't want Felicia going anywhere alone! Do you hear me? Not until I find out more information."

"I had no idea. I'll keep her safe. I promised her that. Keep in touch Jim."

My insides are churning; the thought of anything happening to Felicia makes me want to die. This is fucked up. One man, he's not even a man. He's one disgusting creature taking up space and air on earth and is controlling this whole community. Hell if I'll let that happen.

"Felicia, where are you?"

"I just got home. Why do you sound hyped up?"

"Lock the doors and I'll be there in ten minutes."

"Jake, you're scaring me. What's going on?"

"Angel, don't worry. I promised I would protect you and I will. Just sit tight and I'll be there in a few."

I know that I'm sounding paranoid but with all that has been cropping up I'm out of sorts. I don't like to think that Felicia is alone without protection.

"Felicia, open up! It's Jake!"

As soon as she opened the door I held her so tight. She hugged me back and then pulled away. She is still nursing her delicate wings.

"What the hell is going on Jake? You're scaring the shit out of me."

"Did you know that Harold's cousin owns the Telegram?"

"Yeah, Amanda told me. She was apprehensive at first to run the story but he's out of town on vacation and she said she would take the risk. She also said this was going to be an anonymous tip, not from me."

"That's good news, not great but better than anything I've heard today. There's some funny business going on with the Captain. He's somehow indebted to Harold. I think he might be getting paid by him to mess this case up. Jim told me he lost big money at Foxwoods and his house was up for foreclosure but now it isn't."

"You talked to Jim? When? Was he with Beth? I've been trying to call her all day and left messages and she hasn't called me back."

"I don't know if they were together when we talked. We spoke a short while ago. She's probably busy picking out furniture for the new house they're going to buy."

"Did he say they found a house?"

"No, we didn't talk about that. Jim's going to start work tomorrow and work on this case. He doesn't want you going out alone, just to be cautious. I also think it's a good idea that we move in together sooner than later."

"Jake, who the hell is this guy? I think we stumbled upon more than pedophiles."

"You can say that again. Money is power, that's what I learned more than I care to know about today."

"I have to say, I'm numb. This doesn't even seem real. What about the kids? Are they safe where they are? Who can protect them? It's obvious not our police department?"

"I have a couple friends that I went to the Academy with that are now Private Investigators; I'll give them a call to see if they can help out with that. Maybe stake out or even stay in the houses with the kids."

"Jake, please call! These kids need to be safe."

"One other thing Felicia... have you ever fired a gun?"

"Are you out of your mind? No! I haven't even held one."

"That's going to change but for now; we're getting you some mace."

"You want me to carry a gun? Jesus Jake, I have a hard time stepping on an ant."

"Felicia, I saw you with the Captain. If someone was going to hurt someone you cared about, I think you would find it in yourself to pull the trigger if needed. I'm not saying shoot before you need to but you need to be protected."

"Do you have a gun Jake?"

"Of course I do. I just wish I had one when I was young so I could have put a bullet between my father's eyes before he killed my mother."

"Jake, you never could have killed him. You may have wanted to but I don't think you have it in you. How the hell did the Monroe's get to be foster parents? They never should have made it through the backgrounds?"

"Oh my god Felicia! Do you think? No, can't be."

"What Jake?"

"Do you think that someone at Social Services got paid off by the Monroes to be able to fucking have sex with kids?"

"This is unbelievable. I bet you're right. Jennifer Sanford. You haven't met her. She took an early retirement at 37 years old, about six months ago. She drove a new Mercedes; she wore expensive jewelry and clothes. I always wondered with no husband, how she could afford all of that with a salary the same as mine. Shit, I live in a studio apartment.

"What did she do for the system?"

"She was the one that did the interviewing with the prospective foster parents and did the final approvals. She would've had complete discretion where the Monroe's were concerned. They bought her! That's the only explanation. Who the hell gets to retire at age 37 on a Social Worker's salary? Nobody unless someone is flipping the bill."

"Felicia, this is all making sense now. The Monroe's inherit millions. They give to the charities and businesses to make them look good. They have enough money to buy the town. Everyone thinks they are the pillars of society, foster parents to kids that are in need, donating money for good causes. It's brilliant— in a sick fucking way. Harold Monroe has no idea what's coming his way."

"Jake, I believe we can do this. We can as a team take them down."

"I have to call Jim back and tell him what we just figured out and also ask about any good pro bono attorneys for the kids. Why don't you take a bath while I call Jim?"

"That sounds delightful Jake. Will you join me after? I think you need a little R &R too."

"I will! I love you Felicia."

JAKE

She smiled that beautiful smile back at me and walked into the bathroom and started running a bath. I called Jim and told him about the new developments. He was stunned and he voiced that he was very happy that he was on the other side now so he could help put these bastards away. He told me there were some colleagues of his from the firm he just left that would probably take the kid's cases. He'll check with them in the morning.

I asked him why Beth wasn't answering her phone and told him Felicia was worried. He said they were out looking at houses all day but Beth was afraid she would tell Felicia about David.

She didn't want to worry her until it was a definite. I told Jim the longer Beth doesn't call her the more suspicious she will become that something is wrong. He agreed.

After I hung up with Jim, I ran my hands through my hair and let out a long held in breath. I could smell the lavender seeping under the bathroom door. My beautiful angel is in there, naked and waiting for me. I took off my clothes and set them on the bed, wrapped a towel around my waste and opened the bathroom door.

"Hey Bright Eyes, I've been waiting for you."

Without hesitation, I became hard, dropped the towel and slipped in the tub behind her, pulling her back between my legs.

"Sorry it took so long. Can we not talk while we're in here; I just want to feel you."

"Say no more."

FELICIA

Jake began to massage my neck and shoulders; the tightness in my neck was like the strings in a golf ball. Probably from clenching my jaw all day. He took the bath poof and lathered me up. His touch was gentle and comforting. It was exactly what I needed. When he dripped the sudsy water over my breasts it was soothing. I carefully turned around to face him so I could kiss his lips without drowning.

Complete silence. He looked in my eyes and mine

back at his and we kissed tenderly. Our tears met one another's as our cheeks pressed together. It was a heinous day and we both needed to feel the safety of one another.

I could feel his erection coming back. I placed him inside of me and we made love. With no words, the intimacy was intense. It was exactly what I needed. I hate to sound cliché, but he really does complete me. Actually, more like he has created the new me.

We had to eat. I know I only had a yogurt today and I'm not sure if Jake had anything at all. The bath is empty and it's time to see what I can conjure up in the kitchenette. I told Jake I would cook him dinner but I'm not counting tonight as that dinner. All I'm looking at is Spaghettios and Campbell's Tomato Soup in the cabinets. The refrigerator is offering us cheese, milk, wine and a shriveled up peach.

Grocery shopping hasn't been on my To Do List lately. I found some bread. It will be tomato soup and grilled cheese.

Jake surveyed his eyes over to the stove and smiled.

"You're cooking me dinner?"

"Okay, this isn't *the* dinner that I was going to cook for you but it's what I have. I swear I can cook more than this."

"It's perfect Felicia."

We sat down on the sofa and ate our exquisite meal in front of the television. In all honesty, this meal was comforting to me and Jake seemed to enjoy it as well. We put a movie in; we needed something light and funny after today, so we put in Bridesmaids. Jake had never seen it and thought it to be a chick flick. It is but I bet he'll laugh.

Felicia & Beth

My phone rang; and it's Beth, thank god.

"Hey Beth, where have you been? I've been worried sick about you!"

"Felicia, I'm so sorry! The first time you called I was in a position that I couldn't talk, if you know what I mean. The second time you called, Jim and I were with the realtor. I'm sorry girl."

"You're forgiven. Did you find a house?"

"We did. The first one we saw looked like it was out of the 1960 era, no updates, nothing. The second one, we knew right away that it was our home."

"Congratulations. Where is it?"

"It's on Sutherland Street. It has a great big back yard. A bigger back yard than my non-existent back yard at the apartment. It has a great screened in porch. A fireplace, a kitchen that was built for a chef. Felicia, I don't cook much but even it made me horny. There are four bedrooms, a study, a family room, dining room and a fucking hot tub."

"Sounds to me like you've just found your dream home. When do you move in?"

"We can actually move in two or three weeks, once the inspections are done and such. I'll let you know because we'll need you and Jake's help. We'll make a party out of it."

"That sounds awesome, we're in. Whatever you need us to do."

I can hear Jake laughing in the background; it just came to the part where they were in the Bridal Shop and getting sick. Hysterical.

"How are you doing Felicia? Jim told me he heard from Jake today. Are you okay?"

"Right now I am. I'm looking over at the sofa and this beautiful man is laying down watching Bridesmaids in his boxer shorts."

"He's good for you Felicia. You have a keeper. He adores you and he's not afraid to show it. That says a lot about a guy."

"Well Jim adores you and he shows you."

"Yeah, you're right; I guess we both landed the good

ones. I'm sorry again about not answering but I have to say I'm beat. Are we meeting at the Diner tomorrow?"

"I don't think so. Jim told Jake that I have to keep a low- profile and I'm sure he wouldn't want us meeting alone."

"Maybe you can fill me in on everything in the morning, Jim didn't tell me much."

"Okay Bethy, talk to you in the morning. Please congratulate Jim for me. Good Night, Love you!"

"I love you too girl!"

Everything seemed great with Beth. I worried for nothing. Things are falling into place for her and Jim and I couldn't be happier for them. Jake is cracking up laughing at this movie. I walked the few steps to get to him on the sofa and I kissed him on the forehead.

"Is Beth okay?"

"She's great, they found a house today. It sounds like a dream home. They're moving in two or three weeks and I told her we'd help them. I hope you don't mind."

"That's awesome and of course I don't mind. They're our friends."

I snuggled up next to him and we continued to watch

the movie. When I lay down in his arms, it was lights out for me.

I must say it wasn't a sound sleep, not to mention we were on the sofa and Jake is six foot two and he was very restless all night. I heard him say things in his sleep but I couldn't make it out. He was still sleeping when I woke up and that wasn't usual for him but after yesterday, I know he was beat.

I got up and made some coffee, at least I had that, never did I let myself run out of that. I went and took a shower and got dressed. When I came out of the bathroom, Jake was still sleeping. This time I heard him talking in his sleep, saying, "Daddy, please! I don't like it, don't make me do it again."I didn't want to invade in his privacy but I didn't have any options of rooms to go in this studio. I took my coffee out on the porch and sat and stared at the nature, this is my new relaxation. I saw movement out of the corner of my eye.

It was Jake; he was running to the bathroom. I went inside and I could hear him retching.

"Jake, are you okay in there? Are you sick?"

"Angel, I'm fine. Just an upset stomach."

"Do you want some water?"

"No, I'll be out in a second, thanks though."

After the longest second, he came out sweating and looking defeated.

"I think it was the tomato soup and grilled cheese."

"No Felicia, I'm fine."

"I'm kidding. I'm going to jump in the shower and then we can go over to my place so I can get some clothes."

"Sounds good. You sure you're okay?"

"Yes, I'm fine. Please don't you worry."

After he showered, he made sure the apartment was sealed tight and we went to his place for him to put fresh clothes on. Before he would let me walk in he checked the place out.

"Jake, what are you looking for? Do you really think we're in danger?"

"Felicia, I'd rather be safe than sorry and I told you I would protect you and that's what I'm doing."

"I get it, I'm sorry Jake."

"It's all good. I'm just going to change my clothes and we'll be ready to go to the office."

While he was in his bedroom getting changed, I saw a

picture on the shelf that I hadn't noticed before. It was of Jake and I assume his mom. She was beautiful. She had green-blue eyes like Jake. She was thin and very well kept but she looked tired.

After seeing and hearing Jake, I forgot all about the newspaper. I have no idea what to expect after this hits the shelves and the mailboxes. When we walked into the office it reminded me of a funeral parlor. There were people everywhere, parents and children.

"Felicia, you've got a busy day ahead of you. There are seven foster families here to report abuse from Harold and Cindy Monroe," Erin notified me with a look of panic.

"Jeese, what time does the paper come out," I asked.

"Three in the morning but don't forget the internet version," Erin said reminding me.

"Jake, we have our work cut out for us today. These are all victims of the Monroe's," I said with sadness in my voice.

"This is awful. I say you take the girls and I take the boys," Jake suggested.

"Okay. Are you okay," I agreed.

"I will be when these kids get justice," Jake answered.

"Hello everyone, my name is Felicia Westfield and this is Investigator Jake Brown. I'm so sorry you had to come in today but I'm so happy that you all did. Mr. Brown and I are going to be talking with you all. I'm going to talk with the girls and he will speak to the boys. Please know nobody here is in trouble. You are all very brave. If you give me a minute, I will call you one at a time."

I had a list of six girls and Jake had a list of four boys. Ten more victims and the phone was ringing constantly.

My first girl was only six years old when she lived with the Monroes. She wasn't there long at all; it was a respite situation while they were finding her a permanent placement.

The hours went by like minutes. Each girl had the same story. One became more heartbreaking than the next. I recorded each conversation with each girl to minimize the times they had to tell their story.

Jake had four boys and the youngest being seven at the time of the abuse. Each story was the same as Joey's and Daniel's. Jake got the boys to trust him and tell him everything.

When I finished with my interviews, I walked out of

my office and saw Captain Murphy talking to the families.

"Captain Murphy, can I help you," I asked him with an attitude.

"Miss Westfield, I heard there was some commotion here so I thought I'd better check on it," the Captain answered nervously.

"There's no commotion here, everything is under control. We're doing our jobs. Is that what you're doing? Which job are you doing here today? The job of protecting the innocent or protecting the pedophile?"

"Excuse me Miss Westfield; I don't quite know what you mean."

Jake walked in and saw Captain Murphy and he looked dismayed.

"Cap, what are you doing here," Jake questioned.

"Jake, I heard there was some commotion down here so I came to make sure everything was alright."

"As Miss Westfield said, we're doing our jobs."

"Well, it looks like you have everything under control, carry on. Good day," the Captain says as he begins to walk away.

"Hey Cap, you're no longer involved in this investigation. I advise you to stay out of it for your own good."

"Are you threatening me Jake?"

"No sir, I know you were a good man once. I think it would be best for you and your family to forget this case."

Captain Murphy turned around and walked out.

"Felicia, you are unbelievable. I'm so proud of you."

"Were you there the whole time? I was shaking and I wouldn't have noticed if an elephant had walked in the room."

"I heard enough. How are you holding up?"

"Not sure how to put it... mentally drained, sad, furious, disgusted, scared and sick and did I say angry?"

"That about sums it up for me too."

Jake and I went into the conference room where everyone was waiting after the confrontation with Captain Murphy.

"Okay, I just have to say, I'm so proud of each and every one of you, including the parents. It wasn't easy coming in here today and talking to Miss Westfield and myself. I want you to know that we are doing everything we can to punish Cindy and Harold Monroe and with you all coming down here today and opening up to us. You all just made our job much easier. Miss Westfield and I would like to thank you all and say that you are all heroes. You are helping to make sure these terrible things don't happen to any other child," Jake spoke with care and comfort.

"We'll be in touch with the next steps. Mr. Brown is working with the District Attorney's office and they are putting this case a top priority. Our goal is for all of you children to be able to start putting this behind you and healing from this pain. Not one of you deserved this and this was not your fault," I said trying to reassure these kids.

The kids and adults alike were all wiping tears from their eyes. What a heart-gripping day. There were at least four more kids coming in tomorrow. Anyone that calls in is instructed to come in and not go to the local police. When something happens like this, they must report it to us first and in this case, it will be the District Attorney's office and us.

I wanted to just go home and curl up in a ball and eat Purple Cow but the day isn't over. Jake has to go see Jim at his new office and I have to tag along because he doesn't want me alone. I'm so thankful that Jim got this job and is finally going to put the bad guys away instead of helping them go free.

We got to the office of the District Attorney's; it's

nothing that I had pictured. White walls, no marble flooring, just a regular old office. It just reiterates how less you go with to do the right thing.

"Jake, Felicia, come on in. This is my office, excuse the lack of décor," Jim welcomed us in.

"Jim, it looks like you have all you need right there on your desk. That's a phenomenal picture of Beth," I said looking around.

"Felicia, you know how much of a ham she is in front of a camera. That's one of my all time favorites of her," Jim said smiling as he was thinking back to Beth.

"Jim, we interviewed ten kids today. They all have the same story and details regarding Harold," Jake informed him.

"This is good, not good that it happened to the kids but good that we have more evidence and names to put up on the screen for them to see," said Jim.

"Captain Murphy showed up at our office today and he was speaking with some of the kids. He claims he heard there was commotion going on and he had to check it out," I said with my voice irritated.

"Really? Maybe he's watching things and saw the people going in. Whatever the reason, I don't like it but until we can prove Harold Monroe is paying him off we have to remain civil. I will be getting a warrant for his bank information and I'll be visiting Ms.

Sanford tomorrow as well," Jim talking just like an official ADA.

"Have you had a chance to look into any of your colleagues to represent the kids," I asked.

"Yes. Thanks for reminding me. For the Bishop's I think that Karen Weslo is great and for Daniel, John Croteau. They have both volunteered their services. Beth works closely with these attorneys as she is their investigator," Jim said.

"Thank you Jim. I appreciate everything so far," Jake said, shaking his hand.

"Hey, there's nothing like jumping right in before I start. Jake, this is a giant case and it has to be won. I will do everything in my power to make it in our favor," Jim replied with confidence.

"Here's the box of tapes that we have of all the kids from today and Daniel. Listen with caution, it's not easy listening," I handed him the box.

"Will do. Felicia, how would you feel about Beth meeting with Ms. Sanford? After all she'll be the investigator for the attorneys," Jim asked.

"I think Beth will be perfect. She won't have any problems breaking her down," I said with excitement.

"I think we're heading in the right direction. This case is our top priority. The DNA results will be sent to me and they should be here by Thursday, I had them rush it," Jim said.

"Jim, thank you so much and congratulations on the house," I smiled.

"Thanks, we can't wait to move in and have you over for dinner. Have you started looking for a place to live yet," Jim asked us.

"We haven't yet with all that's been going on but will be sooner than later," Jake said.

"I understand that. I'm glad we found something before your call Jake. I'll be in touch and if you hear from anyone else let me know. That article was fantastic and I won't be surprised if it hits the news tonight," Jim stated.

Jake and I left Jim's office, stopped and got a pizza on the way to his place. It's going to be a quiet night, eat and sleep.

We ate pizza when we got back to Jake's and I went straight to bed. Jake stayed up a bit and watched the news. There it was, on every news station. Pictures of Harold and Cindy Monroe at a benefit for children with the caption under the photo reading:

Pillars of society, in custody for aggravated sexual assault against children.

JAKE

It's all out there now. The reporters were saying how shocked they were and that you just never know. Then they panned the camera on a man and a woman, they looked familiar. It dawned on me, they were little Robbie's foster parents. They had a few choice words to say for Harold and Cindy Monroe. The fight is on and the pillars will be crumbling.

I turned off the television and sat in silence. I needed this silence to think. Visualizing what I would say if I saw him, none of it would be kind but I can't keep having the nightmares. I have to face him and let him know he no longer has power over me. I have a voice and he needs to hear it. Tomorrow after work I'm going to the prison for the first time. Ed Brown will face me for the first time since before he killed my mom. He can no longer hurt me. This has to be done.

FELICIA

I woke up to the sounds again of Jake retching in the bathroom. What's going on? I decided to let him be and wait for him to come out of the bathroom. A few minutes later he surfaced, sweaty and pale again.

"Jake, are you okay?"

"I will be. I will be."

"Jake, I heard you the other night in your sleep, begging to not make you do it again. What was that about?

"Felicia, there's something I need to tell you."

"What is it? Whatever it is; I'm here for you Jake."

"Felicia, I'm no different than Joey, Daniel and the other boys. My father made me do it to him. I've had nightmares for years and it keeps replaying in my head. Since these boys have come forward, I can't get the vision out of my head. I'm going to see my father tomorrow in prison; I have to take back the power. Will you come with me?"

"Jake, I'm so sorry. You do know that it wasn't in your control right? Of course I'll go with you. I'm so proud of you. I love you no matter what."

"Felicia, he's had control over me since he started beating me and that other stuff. I can't do it anymore; it's time to set myself free."

"I'm right here for you. He can't hurt you anymore. It's over; remember the Maple Leaf will help get rid of Demons."

I held him in my arms and rocked him back and forth like a baby. At this time; he was like an innocent baby that needed his mommy after he skinned his knees for the first time. This tall, beautiful man has been diminished to a young scared child. Feeling like the one that's done wrong. I held him until he fell back asleep. I stayed awake most of the night looking down at him and praying for closure. This beautiful man was stuck inside of an adult body but it seems he's a defenseless little boy inside. Praying that tomorrow will help him become all that he should be…FREE!

After finally falling asleep for about an hour, I woke up to find the bed empty next to me. I got up and walked into the kitchen where Jake was making pancakes and singing. I didn't know he could sing. He looked much better than he did last night.

"Good morning Angel."

"Good morning to you Bright Eyes. You seem chipper this morning."

"Today is a new day! A long overdue day to confront my demons. Felicia, I'm sorry about last night. I just thought it was time for you to know I have nightmares since we'll be sharing a bed."

"Oh Jake, never apologize for being human. I'm so glad you told me. Do you at least feel better this morning after getting that off your chest?"

"Felicia, I've never told anyone what my father made me do to him. Oddly, I feel better and more prepared to see him today."

"Jake, this is another step that needs to be taken for your soul to heal and I'm by your side through it all. Are you heating up the maple syrup for me?"

"Yes I am. Come over here and kiss me."

I stepped towards him and he pulled me to him. His eyes were upon me and I actually could see relief in them. He leaned down, touched his fingers to my lips like a feather and brought his lips to mine. This kiss was more than a kiss, it was a kiss filled with love, trust, need and forever.

"If you keep kissing me like that, we'll never get to work on time."

"Felicia, I would like nothing more than to kiss you all day like that and forget about the day ahead of us. We have too many kids that need us today, so I wanted you to think of that kiss all day."

"I think I'll think of that kiss for the rest of my life."

My phone rang, it was Beth for our morning coffee talk. She was going to do a surprise visit with Jennifer Sanford today.

"Good Morning Beth."

"Good Morning to you girl."

Finding Home

"Beth, promise me you'll be careful today."

"I'm always careful; she'll be putty in my hands when I'm done with her. Plus, I'll have my piece with me if it gets out of hand."

"You have a gun? How come you never told me that?"

"I've had one for years. I have to for my job; I don't meet with the cream of the crop often."

"Jake is making me get a gun and I'm not feeling it."

"Knowing you have that to protect yourself Felicia, is peace of mind. With everything that's going on, I think Jake's right."

"Maybe you both are right. I'll have to get used to it, I guess. Jake and I are going to the prison today to see his father. He's ready to confront him."

"Holy Shit girl, that's huge. Good for him. It's time he lets that bastard know what he thinks of him."

"He's having nightmares and after all that we both have heard from these kids, I think he realizes that he has to be brave and do this to fully move on."

"Call me later and let me know how it goes and I'll fill you in on Ms. Sanford. This is a good thing Felicia and with you by his side he'll be able to get through it."

"Thanks Beth, I'll talk to you later."

When Jake and I arrived at the office, it was more of the same as yesterday. More kids and more broken souls. Today I saw three girls. They are now teenagers. Jake saw another four boys, which brings the count to seventeen.

It was another brutal day. Jake and I met in my office after our interviews; we had to steal a quiet moment. We just hugged one another and were interrupted by Jake's phone ringing.

JAKE & JIM

"Jake Brown."

He walked out of my office and into his and closed the door.

"Jake it's Jim; I just got the DNA back. It's a match! A perfect fucking match. Harold Monroe will be spending years behind bars and getting fucked up the ass like he did to those kids."

"I smell Justice Jim. We have seven more kids to add to the list so far today."

"The arraignment has been set up for tomorrow. I'm going to have great pleasure delivering what I think is fair and just."

"Thank you Jim. Maybe this nightmare will finally come to an end."

"There's one more thing Jake. When Beth went to visit Ms. Sanford earlier, she banged on the door for a while, but no answer. Her Mercedes was in the driveway and her cat was meowing at the side door. Beth could see a reflection through the window and didn't like what she thought she saw. I called it in and the police went over and broke down the door. Jennifer Sanford hung herself."

"Holy Shit! That's awful; she must have had a conscience."

"I'm sure she saw the newspaper and the news and realized it was her that allowed this to happen. I have no sympathy for her. She got what she deserved."

"I guess you're right. Justice comes in all forms. How's Beth after seeing that?"

"She's a bit shaken up; it's not every day you find someone hanging from the ceiling. She's tough, she'll get through it. I'll make sure of it. Maybe we could meet for dinner tonight; it would help Beth a lot."

"I'm not sure tonight will be good. Felicia and I are driving out to the prison in a little bit. I'm going to see my father for the first time since he murdered my mother. It's time to take back power from him. I can't seem to completely move forward and if these kids can come forward, I can certainly face that devil that has had a hold over me for far too long."

"Jake, I wish you luck with that. I think you're doing the right thing. It's time we all face our demons and move forward. Let me know if you need anything, Beth and I are here for you two always."

"Maybe we could go down to the Cape this weekend; we could all use a change of scenery."

"That sounds perfect. I'll have Beth get us a place. Hey Jake, this is all going to work out."

"I hope you're right Jim. I'll talk to you later."

Jim and I hung up the phone and I sat back in my chair and thought about everything he just told me. There was nothing really to smile about but it was beginning to look like things would go in these kids' favor.

I grabbed my phone, my briefcase and went to Felicia's office to tell her it was time to go. She was sound asleep with her head on the desk. I must have kept her up all night last night. I stood there and kept saying, I'm so sorry Angel. I went and kissed her cheek and she woke up.

"Where am I? Oh my god, I fell asleep."

"You're in your office Angel. I'm so sorry you didn't sleep last night."

"Wow, I've never done that before. It's not your fault Jake. Are you ready to go?"

"I'm as ready as I'll ever be."

"I'm going to run to the bathroom before we leave. Can you grab us some sodas from the machine?"

"Sure. Felicia, thank you."

"You're welcome. I'm confused at why you are thanking me?"

"Without ever meeting you I don't think I would have the courage to go to that prison."

"You would have when the time was right. I think now it's just the right time for you."

FELICIA & BETH

On the ride there. I called Beth. I was beyond curious to find out how her meeting with Jennifer went today.

"Beth, are you busy?"

"No, I'm home and trying to get the vision out of my head."

"Vision of what? Are you okay? Did you see a hairy spider?"

"Jake didn't tell you?"

"Jake didn't tell me what?"

Jake looked over at me when he heard me and mouthed, "I'm sorry."

"I went to Jennifer Sanford's house and she was hanging from the ceiling. Dead!"

"Holy Fuck Beth. Are you okay?"

"I'm better than she is but I'm a bit freaked out. At least we know she was the one and guilty as sin."

"Funny thing is, I feel bad that you had to find her. Not that she is dead, she deserves it."

"I'll be fine, really. Jim's going to pamper me. I might just milk it for a while."

We both laughed.

"We're almost to the prison. I'll call you later."

"Stay strong for him Felicia. This is a good thing."

"I know it is and I will. Love you."

"Love you too girl."

JAKE & FELICIA

"Felicia, I'm sorry I didn't tell you. I went to your office to tell you but you were asleep and then my thoughts got away from me. Crazy shit huh?"

"For sure. She got what she deserved. It's one less
sicko that we have to go after. I just wish
Beth didn't have to find her."

"Yeah, Jim said she was pretty shaken up but he was
going to take good care of her."

In our view were guards accompanying the high metal
fence with electric wires on the top and the lookout
tower. We are here. I can see Jake's hands shaking a
bit and I grab a hold of it squeeze to let him know it'll
be okay.

After we parked the car we had to walk a ways to get
to the entrance and that meant we had to walk by the
prisoners in the yard. Some were chanting things to
me and my skin was crawling with the heebie jeebies. I
heard my name called all of a sudden. I stopped in my
tracks and turned to the yard. Jake was pulling my
hand and not wanting me to stop.

David. It was David. My body began to tremble and I
nearly passed out. Jake held me up and pulled me as
close to him as possible and we continued to walk to
the entrance.

"Felicia, he can't hurt you. He's locked up in there."

"I had no idea he was in this prison. Just seeing him
again makes me feel weird. I never thought I would
see him again."

"After today, you won't ever see him again."

"Let's hope not."

Jake went up to the check in counter, if that's even what they call it and told the guard whom he was here to see. His voice was low and cracking as he spoke, Edward Brown. I could see in his eyes that it was like all the memories were flashing before him. The same thing is happening to me in this moment after hearing and seeing David.

"Jake, I need to go to the ladies room. Can you wait here a minute?"

"Are you okay Felicia? I know seeing David isn't something you expected."

"I'm fine; I just have to go to the bathroom."

The bile is making its way into my throat before I reach the bathroom door. Trying to be strong and act as though seeing David doesn't bother me. I opened the door and went into the first stall. The toilet hadn't even been flushed but it was coming and I can't stop it. There was no time to waste. Every memory came back to me as I purged the contents of my stomach in the dirty toilet. I could hear Beth's voice in my head now telling me, "it's in the past and he can't hurt you ever again." I realize at that moment, I just found life and love and I couldn't live in the past any longer. At this moment, I am purging it all. My body is still trembling but I have to make a choice. The choice I must choose is to leave the past where it belongs, in the past. I just found myself again. I can't let the vision of David cloud me and put me back in the numb state. I walked back to Jake where he was waiting to be escorted to see his father. Still shaken a bit but for the first time I know I have someone to turn to.

"Angel, are you okay? You look very pale."

"I am much better now. I guess seeing David made me feel sick."

"Mr. Brown, you two can come back now. He'll be behind the glass so there's no physical contact."

"Thank you."

"He's in the second cubicle waiting."

Jake looked at me and I squeezed his hand and we both walked slowly to the second cubicle. Jake didn't take a step right away; he was sizing his father up. His father was a handsome man but with dark and hollow eyes.

JAKE'S FATHER

"Jake, what brings you here? Did you come to say you're sorry for being such a pansy," Jake's father ridiculed.

I couldn't keep my mouth shut.

"Mr. Brown, you don't know anything about this man in front of you. He is strong and caring and the only pansy I see is you. You are a weak man, Mr. Brown. You beating on a woman and a young boy, your own blood for Cripes Sake, nonetheless. The man you see before you, you have nothing that he possesses," I scorned at him.

"Got yourself a little firecracker don't you Jake. She's hot too but with that mouth, you'll be beating her in no time son," Jake's father laughed.

"Don't you ever call me that again! I'm not your son. I am not a coward like you. I would never raise my hand to a woman. That's your style, not mine," Jake raised his voice.

"You wait and see Jake. So are you hear to gloat," Jake's father asked.

"No, I'm here to tell you that you no longer have power over me. You are a disgrace to the human race. I've built my life to help put scumbags like you away. You will never hurt me again and I hope that you rot in here. I hope that you have been raped in here, as you did to me. But you know what? I'm good now. You're nothing to me, not even a memory. Felicia and I are going to get married and be happy and I will never hurt her like you did my mother."

"Jake, your mother was a pain in the ass and she deserved everything she got," his father said proudly.

"Listen you fucking asshole… my mother was the kindest, most giving woman and she didn't deserve what you did to her. You didn't know how to handle such greatness because you were such a failure. You have never been a man. You are a weak, sick Fuck that got his rocks off causing others pain. That ends today; never will you cause me another minute of pain. You are a worthless piece of shit."

"Son, this meeting is over. Guard, I'm done here."

"What's the matter Mr. Brown, can't handle the truth? Maybe you do have a conscience buried deep in that warped mind of yours," Felicia couldn't hold back.

"Don't ever come back here Jake," Jake's father shouted.

"You don't have to worry about that. I hope you rot in hell. Oh and by the way, just because your sperm mixed with my mother's egg it doesn't make you a father. Let's go Felicia."

What a despicable man. I really hope Jake got what he came for. This man doesn't deserve to be in Jake's head.

We had to walk by the yard again, praying that David is no longer outside. Jake held my hand as we walked swiftly past. The voice, that voice I'll never forget was louder and closer than before.

"Felicia, see you soon," David yelled out.

Jake went up to the fence, as close as he could without getting zapped. He looked David square in the eye and said, "You will never see her again, you bastard. Run along and play with your friends you prick."

"Hey pretty boy…don't count on it," David said speaking through the fence with empty and dangerous eyes.

I couldn't stay silent anymore. If David is at the fence, he is obviously opening himself up.

"David, how's life treating you behind those bars? It's beautiful on the outside. The grass is green, the birds are singing and there's love in the air. It looks like you didn't do enough for me to not find love. You are a nothing David. Let me tell you this, Jake here, he makes me scream with pleasure. I hope at least the guys up your ass are giving you pleasure," I proudly said.

"You little whore! If I were you I'd watch your back," David responded with anger.

"Whatever David, you can never take from me what I have now. Go on behind the bars, that's where you belong just like a rabid animal," I shouted.

We walked away as fast as we could, trying to drown out the sound of David's voice still yelling to me. Jake opened the car door for me and squeezed my hand before he shut the door. He got in and sped out of the lot. He drove for a few miles and then pulled to the side of the road.

"Felicia, if I had known he was at the same prison I never would have had you come with me."

"Oddly, I'm okay. I can't say that it didn't give me pleasure seeing him locked up like a dog in training. He's got a lot of time left to serve; I can't let him get the best of me."

"How do you still amaze me? Your mother must have been one strong lady to have a daughter like she has; she must be looking down at you and beaming with pride."

"My mother had such strength and fight in her. I'd be proud to be like my mother. How are you feeling after seeing your father?"

"I got to him. For the first time in my life, I got to him. If I hadn't, he never would've ended the visit. I feel good. I feel relief that I'm nothing like him. He's cold and lacks feeling; he's no longer a part of me."

I never even noticed that he was driving again. I felt the same as Jake at this moment. I got to David and it felt damn good.

"Jake, I think we should celebrate. We should call Beth and Jim and see if they want to go to dinner."

"Jim asked me earlier but I told him not tonight. I'm sorry. Tonight I just want to be with you. However, we're all going to the Cape for the weekend. Beth is supposed to be setting everything up. It'll be great getting away, walking the beach with you."

"I'm so excited. I can think of a bit more I'd like to do on the beach with you." Felicia smiled.

"I'm glad to hear that because I have a lot more planned for you and I on the beach."

We both were finally smiling. After the day we had, who would have thought a smile could form. All those precious kids coming forward, the prison, David, Ed Brown, this stuff isn't in your average day but it's our reality lately.

"Hey Jake, do you think I could go shopping with Beth tomorrow after work? I'd like to get a few things for the weekend. She carries a piece, so we'll be fine."

"Beth is packing? See… you can do it. Once we get to the target range you'll be packing a piece too. That sounds like fun for the two of you. I think things will settle down now. Go shopping and maybe Jim and I will play racquetball."

"I have to call her; she'll be excited to bring me to her shops."

"What kind of shops are those?"

Finding Home

"The kind that I'm embarrassed to walk into."

"Sounds intriguing."

We both laughed as we turned the corner to Jake's place. Suddenly feeling more relaxed than I have in a while. Jake looks like he is too, his eyebrows aren't stuck anymore.

As we're walking in to the apartment, my phone rang. I looked at the number and I didn't recognize it.

"Hello, Felicia Westfield."

"Miss Felicia, its Kayla. I'm sorry to call you but I couldn't stop myself."

"Kayla, is something wrong honey?"

"No, well maybe. I got a kitten and I don't know what to name her."

"Honey that's awesome. I know how much you like kittens. What color is she?"

"She's gray and with white paws. She purrs loud and chases her tail."

To hear the happiness in her voice warms my heart and I can't stop the tears.

"How about if I come by tomorrow and visit with you all and we can think of a name?"

"Really, will you please? Can Jake come too?"

"I think we can arrange that. I'll see you tomorrow Kayla."

"I can't wait."

JAKE & FELICIA

"Jake that was Kayla. She got a kitten and she's so happy. She wants us to stop by tomorrow and see her and help name the kitty."

"I was going to the arraignment, we can go over after. Jim said it would be quick, the evidence is against them," Jake said.

"That sounds good. I can't wait to see them."

"You really love those kids huh? I feel the same way about them."

"I do. Kayla's as close to a daughter as I'll ever have."

"Why do you say that, Angel?"

"Jake, you know I can't have kids."

"Maybe not give birth but that surely doesn't mean we can't have kids. We can adopt Felicia. We can give a baby a life that someone couldn't."

A smile gleamed across my face. I could be a mom. A

mom doesn't just mean giving birth. There's so much more to being a mom than that. Jake wants to adopt. I love this man more and more every day.

"Jake, I'd love to adopt. Maybe if we get married sometime we can look into it."

"We'll be married. That isn't a question in my mind. There's nobody in the world I want to spend my life with but you."

"So sweet, I feel the same."

JAKE & JIM

Jake's phone rings.

"Jake Brown."

"Jake, its Jim; sorry to bother you. Amanda Styles from the Telegram is missing. She hasn't shown up for work since the article came out."

"You're kidding me."

"I wish I was. I need to know if Felicia has spoken with her since the article went to print."

"Okay, hold on. Felicia, have you spoken to Amanda Styles since she ran the article?"

"No, I haven't had time to call her and thank her for printing it."

"Jim, she hasn't. Maybe she went on vacation?"

"Don't think so, one of her coworkers said that she got a phone call the morning the article ran and she was upset and ran out of the office."

"Interesting. Is her boss back in town?"

"We're trying to locate him now. Do the kids have some security?"

"I've been so swamped with all these other interviews, I put a call out to two former cops I went to the Academy with and I never called them back. Shit, I'll call them right now. Felicia and I are going to the Bishop's tomorrow."

"Call those guys and call me back. I need to know they are protected."

JAKE

I hung up the phone and immediately called Paul Johnson.

"Hey Paul, its Jake. You got my message. I haven't had time to call back but I need this detail to start immediately. There's been a new development."

I filled Paul in on everything that is happening and he agreed to go stay with the Bishop kids. He'll be better suited for them than Sean Knight. He has a great personality and he looks like a big teddy bear.

"I'll head over now Jake, don't worry. I will keep them all safe."

"Thanks man, I owe you."

"Sean, its Jake. There have been some new developments, any way you can start tonight?"

"Yeah, I cleared everything when I got your message. I saw the news and figured you were busy, so I've been waiting on go."

I briefed Sean on everything, gave him the address and he's good to go.

"Thanks Sean, you're the best."

Felicia is making omelets for dinner and they smell fabulous. I'll have to heat mine up. Have to call the Harpers and the Anthony's and let them know they'll be having a houseguest.

"Jessica, this is Jake Brown. I'm sorry to disturb you but I have to tell you that someone will be knocking at your door soon. He's a private investigator and his name is Paul. He's a great guy and I know him well."

"Why is he coming here?"

"He's coming to stay for a bit. There's been some things happening and we just want to be cautious and keep all of you safe. Paul will fill you both in. I have to go and call another family. Sorry to be so abrupt Jessica, but I have no choice."

"Okay Jake, thank you."

"Felicia and I will see you tomorrow for the kitten naming."

"Yes, that's right. Okay than, good night."

"Hello Geremy, this is Jake Brown."

"Hi Jake, what can we do for you?"

"You will have a man knocking at your door shortly. His name is Sean and he's a private investigator. He's coming to stay with you for a bit."

"What are you talking about Jake?"

"Geremy, there's been some developments and we are taking every precaution we can to protect Daniel and your family. Sean's a great guy and he'll fill you in when he gets there."

"Are we in danger?

"We don't think so but we aren't positive. This is the best way to keep all of you safe."

"I think he's ringing the doorbell now, thanks for the notice Jake."

"Be in touch Geremy."

JAKE & JIM

"Jim, its Jake. Paul Johnson is the PI that will be staying at the Harper's with the Bishop kids. Sean Knight is the PI that will be staying at the Anthony's house with Daniel. They were a bit shocked but seemed okay with it."

"Thanks Jake. I think we can all sleep easier knowing they have someone there looking out for them."

"What are you not telling me Jim?"

"It's Harold Monroe's cousin, Frank Monroe. We haven't located him yet but from what we have learned so far, he's a puppet for Harold. Harold owns this guy and we aren't certain if Harold has given him any orders."

"Is this Frank a dangerous guy? Does he have any priors?"

"The only thing we have on him is driving with a taillight out. He's clean as a whistle. We got a hold of his bank accounts today and either The Telegram sells a shitload of papers or someone is depositing money into his account every week of $10,000. Since Harold has been in custody that number has doubled. We can assume he upped the ante to secure that the paper wouldn't run the story."

"Does this Frank have a family?"

"He has a wife and two daughters."

"What do you know about Harold and Frank's relationship when they were younger?"

"We haven't had much time to delve in that far. Your wheels are turning Jake, what's on your mind?"

"What if Harold sexually molested Frank when they were younger and he is paying him to keep the secret?"

"Son of a bitch Jake, I think you may have just nailed it. It makes perfect sense."

"We need to find him; we need to flip over every stone until we find him. I think I'll pay a visit to The Telegram tomorrow maybe Beth can join me. The answers may lie there."

"Jake, there may just be a job opening for you here at DA's office soon."

"Can't do it man, too busy saving the children. Felicia and Beth are going shopping tomorrow after work, you up for some racquetball?"

"I think I could work off a bit of steam on the court, sure."

"How about we meet at 6:00."

"Sounds great."

"I better get going; my omelet is probably more like a bowl of jello by now."

"Good work Jake. You and Beth will make a great team."

"I'm sure she can teach me a few things."

"She teaches me new things every day, she's a sharp one."

JAKE

We both laughed and hung up the phone. Felicia was asleep on the couch, looking as angelic as ever. I heated up the omelet and I must say it's pretty good.

Was Jim serious about a job at his office? Would I even consider it if he was? It could be a great opportunity and lord knows more money. Something to ponder.

My gut is telling me this Frank Monroe is not a danger. He's a victim. I hope I'm right because we can all sleep a bit easier if that is the case.

I can't help but just watch Felicia sleep. She's so peaceful and beautiful. I can see her as a mother and an amazing mother at that.

I hope I can sleep through the night tonight without any invasions in my dreams. The scars will never leave, but I took the power back and I do feel different in a great way.

JAKE

I can't believe I slept through the alarm. Holy shit! I slept through the night. Halleluiah as Felicia says.

"Felicia, wake up! We're running late! I slept through the alarm."

Rubbing her eyes, she looked adorable with her dried drool on her cheek.

"Did you have another bad night Jake? Is that why you didn't hear the alarm?"

"No, I slept through the night. All night for the first time in several years."

"You sure are bright eyes this morning Jake. I'm so

happy for you."

"C'mon, we're going to have to shower together to save time."

"Do you really think that will save time?"

"What did you have in mind Angel?"

"Start the shower and I'll show you."

I could wake up like this every morning. His eyes had a sparkle in them that I wish I could keep there forever. We took a shower among other things. Jake dropped me off at the office and he left for the arraignment.

"All Rise. The Honorable Judge Toomey presiding."

There aren't many people in the courtroom. As far as spectators, I see a familiar face, an adoptive parent of one of the victims. I caught her eye and gave her a reassuring nod.

"Your honor, the charges against Mr. Harold Monroe are as follows:

- Thirteen counts of felonious sexual assault and we expect more
- Thirteen counts of child abuse
- Bribery
- Coercion
- Criminal Threatening

We ask the court to deny bail as Mr. Monroe poses a flight risk and he is a danger to our society.

"Mr. Monroe, how do you plead?"

"Not guilty."

"Your honor, the charges against Mrs. Cindy Monroe are as follows:

- Thirteen counts of Felonious Sexual Assault with more expected
- Child Abuse
- Child Neglect
- Criminal Threatening

Your honor, we ask that Mrs. Monroe's bail be denied as well due to the severity of these crimes and her flight risk.

"How do you plead Mrs. Monroe?"

"Not Guilty."

Attorney Mason is the defense attorney for Mr. and Mrs. Monroe; he's a high profile attorney with not many losses under his belt.

"Your honor, I would ask that Mr. and Mrs. Monroe be granted bail on their record of contributing to the community and dedicating their lives to help others."

"Court will resume after a ten minute recess. All Rise."

Dedicating their lives to help others my ass. Lock them up and throw away the key. This infuriates me. Jim came over and said he had a good feeling about this and Judge Toomey is a grandfather. That made me feel a tad better but I won't feel relief until I hear no bail.

"All Rise."

"Mr. Monroe and Mrs. Monroe, these are very serious allegations. Having wealth does not make one a pillar of society or immune to the law. I hereby deny bail. Court is adjourned."

"All Rise."

Thank you god is all I can say. Leaving the courthouse, I can't help but think about David's eyes through the prison fence. I can't let Felicia know that he is up for parole. I feel like I'm lying to her and I hate it but I can't have her feel intimidated. Today was a score for the kids. I have to celebrate that.

I arrived back at the office and saw Felicia talking with Erin. I stopped in my tracks and just stared at the magnificence of her beauty. Her strength and resolve is something I admire about her. This weekend I'm going to show her how much I love her.

"Hey Jake, I didn't see you standing there," I said surprised.

"I was just admiring the view," Jake said with his gleaming smile.

"Erin, you should probably know that Jake and I are together," I told her.

"Felicia, I may not be a world scholar but I'm surely not blind. The way you two look at each other makes me envious. I'm happy for you both," Erin said.

"Thanks Erin."

"Felicia, are you ready to go name a kitten," Jake asked playfully.

"Yes, I can't wait to see them. Have a good one Erin."

"You too, love birds," Erin smiled.

I was surprised Erin figured it out; I didn't know we looked at each other a certain way. Today was another busy day with more kids coming forward. I can't wait until tomorrow when we leave for the Cape. I can't wait to hug Kayla, Joey and Adam either.

"Felicia, good news at the arraignment, no bail," Jake said excitedly.

"Hallelujah! Finally something going right," I replied.

"How many more came in today," Jake asked, hoping the answer was zero.

"Two girls, they're sisters and they were the first kids they had. They were six and eight at the time. They were there for only two weeks while their foster parents had to go out of town. Their foster parents adopted them. They're sixteen and eighteen now," I told him.

"They've kept that secret for ten years," Jake sadly said.

"Of course they threatened to kill their foster parents, knowing full well they were going to be adopted." I spitted out with anger.

"Well, the only thing that's going to hurt anymore is his ass in prison. I hope some Big Bertha gets her hands on Cindy and shows her what it's like to be violated and controlled," Jake said with a half smile of justice.

The thought of that makes us laugh and have pleasure, an eye for an eye. We're just about at the Harper's. We rang the doorbell and behind the door, we could hear the kids squealing. Paul answered the door. Jake was right, he is like a big teddy bear.

"Hey Paul, good to see you. Thanks so much for being here," Jake shook his hand.

"I may just end up staying. They have a great pool and Jessica cooks a mean breakfast and the kids are awesome," Paul said.

"Adam, hey champ how are you? Give me a famous Adam hug," I smiled as he jumped in my arms.

"Miss Felicia, you look pretty. It's fun here. I like sharing a room with Joey," Adam said with expression.

"I'm so happy Adam," I said.

"Kayla, Joey, how about a hug," I begged.

Great big hugs all around. Joey of course went to Jake first, then to me. Kayla gave me a huge hug.

"Kayla, you look so beautiful. Did you braid your own hair," I asked her feeling warmth surround me.

"No, Lucy did it for me. She does all kinds of things with hair. I think she'll be a hairdresser when she grows up," Kayla said with such happiness.

"That sounds fantastic Kayla. Where is this little kitty," I asked looking around.

Adam ran and got her. She was with Lucy in her room. Kayla wanted to surprise me with her. This house is full of love. These kids seem happier than they've ever been. Jake took Joey in the front yard to play catch.

"Adam, give me the kitty please," Kayla motioned to him.

"Miss Felicia, look at her paws. They're like socks.

Finding Home

Isn't she so cute," Kayla said with love.

"She's adorable, why don't you name her socks," I suggested.

"Can we think of some more too? Let me call Lucy down, I want her to help us," Kayla saying, having a hard time containing her excitement.

Kayla is adapting so well and it seems that she and Lucy have really hit it off. Lucy came down with her hair done just like Kayla's, very cute.

"Hi Lucy, how are things going with your new house guests," I asked.

"We have a lot of them. I love it and that Paul guy is really funny too," Lucy says laughing.

"I'm glad you like all these people here," I said.

"C'mon Miss Felicia, think... this kitten needs a name and every name I come up with reminds me of bad things. I want her to have a good name," Kayla said with a hint of sadness.

"Okay, here I go. Mittens. Cutie. Smokey. Angel. Gummy Bear. Mia. Faith. Nala. That's a start; do you like any of them, "I rambled.

"I like them all. Gummy Bear, you're funny Miss Felicia but I can't call her that, I eat them. I can't choose," Kayla says, nearly busting at the seams.

"How about if we put the names in a hat and pick from there," I suggested.

"Okay," said Kayla.

Mrs. Harper brought over a bowl, some paper and a pen to write the names. We folded the papers and Lucy was in charge of shaking the bowl and Kayla would pick. Kayla reached her hand in the bowl and grabbed a folded piece of paper.

"What is it? What's the kitty's new name," I asked.

"Faith," Kayla answered with a glowing smile.

"Kayla, I think that's perfect. She looks like a Faith," I said.

"Thank you so much Miss Felicia. I'm going to run upstairs with Lucy, we're doing our nails. I love you," Kayla said while hugging me.

"I love you too Kayla, have fun. See you soon," I said smiling with a full heart watching how happy and excited she was.

She ran up the stairs and my heart filled with joy. Adam went outside to join the boys playing catch and Paul did too. I sat down with Jessica and had some iced tea.

"How are things going Jessica," I asked.

"Good, really good. These are great kids. They have manners and are polite. Kayla can be more of a mom to Adam and Joey at times, but I've talked with her and told her it was her time to be a kid now. She seems to be adapting to that very well," Jessica said.

"How's Joey doing?"

"He's had some nightmares but he recovers quickly. He and my husband spend a lot of time together along with Adam. Joey even asked if he could call him dad."

"This is wonderful news, I can't thank you enough. How's Adam doing, he seems happy."

"Adam is my shadow. He follows me everywhere and always wants to help in the kitchen. He is a precious one for sure. We just love all three of them and we are considering adopting them."

I began to cry, I couldn't help it. These kids have found home, just like Jake, Daniel, and me too.

"Jessica, this is amazing news. It's a lot to take on though, so take your time about it."

"We will!"

"How's it been with Paul here? We think everything will be okay but we just can't take any chances."

"We'd like to adopt Paul too; he's amazing with the

kids."

"Jake said he's a great guy. I think I should go check on the boys."

I went outside and there was no more catch being played the boys were being tickled and laughing so hard. It was a glorious sound.

"Jake, we should get going," I hollered to him.

Watching Jake with these boys made me really want to adopt a baby with him. He'll be an awesome dad. Paul came over to me and said, "Felicia, you have a great man here. He's a diamond in the rough."

"Boy do I know that Paul."

"He looks peaceful, Felicia. He's carried so much with him in his life but he looks at peace and happy now. I can imagine you have a lot to do with that," Paul said sincerity.

"I'd like to think so. I think we both have found where we belong and have changed a bit of how we look at things, in light of everything that has been going on."

"Well, whatever it is, keep on doing it. It's working for you both."

Jake and I said our good-bye's and are going to Jake's place. Beth's picking me up soon and she'll be corrupting me. Jake and Jim are playing racquetball.

I'm so glad they hit it off. This truly has been one of the better days lately. Kayla, Joey, Adam and Faith all look content and happy. This is a gift.

"Felicia, the kids looked amazing, didn't they? All smiles and feeling at home," Jake said with a content look in his eye.

"It goes to show sometimes you have to go through crap to find what you've been missing."

"So true."

"I can't wait to have some girl time with Beth. I say that now but I could regret it later. She will have me trying on things I would never dream on putting on my body."

"You could come home with a roll of cellophane and I'd think you were beautiful."

"Don't say that. What she picks out will probably be close to that."

When we got to Jake's I changed and put on a pair of Levi's. I'm happy that I brought some clothes over the other day. Jake came out of the bedroom with a pair of black nylon shorts and a light blue t-shirt and he was smoking hot.

Jake wouldn't leave until Beth came. Therefore, I thought while we were waiting, I would give him an appetizer of what was to come when I got home. He was sitting on the couch, bending over tying his shoe when I got behind him and nuzzled into his neck. Whispering in his ear, things he never expected.

He pulled me from behind onto his lap and kissed me ferociously. He was now peeking out of his shorts. Than the doorbell rang. I laughed and he couldn't stand up to say hello.

Leaving him like that made for a great night tonight when I got home. Beth and I left and Jake was to follow.

FELICIA & BETH

"Are you ready girl? Tonight you are stepping outside of your comfort zone," Beth asked with that voice she has when she's up to something.

"Do I have a choice?"

"Nope. This is so fun; it seems like forever that we've had girl time."

"You can say that again. Everything is changing so fast Beth. You and Jim are buying a house. I found a man that I only thought I would know in my dreams. It's all good but it's so different. I feel alive again. Even after I saw him yesterday. I was okay after a while."

"Everything is changing Felicia, but you know it comes when it's right and this is your time and my time too. Who did you see yesterday?"

"David."

"He's out already? Where the hell did you see him?"

"At the prison when we went to see Jake's dad. He said he would see me soon. He's got two and half more years in there before I have to worry about that."

"Let's not even talk about him, this is our night!"

"You're right. I want to get something really cute to wear at the Cape. I'm thinking yellow, a pale yellow sundress."

"Sounds too pure to me. Now that I know you're getting some I'm making you sexy it up a bit. I'm hooking you up Tattoo girl, just follow my lead."

"Lead the way."

JAKE

Jim and I met at the bar to grab a quick bite before hitting the court. It felt good sipping a cold one with a friend. I told him how we saw David yesterday and he still hadn't heard about his parole. We talked about the women in our lives and had a few laughs.

"Jim would you mind taking a pit stop before we go to the court?"

"No problem, where are you thinking?"

"I have to pick something up at the jewelers."

"No way Jake. Are you proposing?"

"Indeed I am. I'm planning on this weekend at the Cape."

"That makes two of us."

"No shit Jim, do you want me to wait?"

"Of course not. This is perfect for the girls."

"As long as you're sure? You guys have been together so much longer than Felicia and I. I don't want to ruin the stage for Beth, you know."

"Believe me Jake, Beth and Felicia would want it this way. They'd want to getting married on the same day and have a baby on the same day. Oh sorry, that was insensitive of me, I forgot about Felicia."

"No worries. We're talking about adopting. These girls sound like they are twins."

"I think they wish they were but funny thing is, they are complete opposites. Felicia, she's conservative, reserved and Beth, she's out there but I love her."

"I've seen Felicia pretty feisty man. Not in the way you think. She went straight in the Captain's face and to my fuck up father."

"I did notice she was more outgoing when we were at dinner and much more expressive. I think since she met you she has revived."

"She's someone I never thought I would ever find. Damn glad I did. She's not the only one that has revived. Let's get out of here before I turn into a complete sap."

Jim and I walked down the block to the jewelry store to pick up the ring for Felicia. I wanted to give her my mom's ring but it was from a monster. Instead, I picked out what I think she will love. An antique solitaire in platinum. It's precious, just like her.

I couldn't show Jim the ring; I wanted Felicia to see it first. We picked it up and decided we needed to celebrate instead of playing racquetball, so we went back to the bar.

FELICIA & BETH

"Felicia, you look fantastic in that! Jake will have that off of you in no time."

"I don't look like a slut?

"No girl, you look sexy. It's okay to look a little slutty once in a while with your man. They like it. Next stop is the toy store."

"Beth, you're killing me. I can't walk in there."

"Yes you can. Jim and I use them all the time. It makes things more fun when you've hit the plateau that we all do."

I have to say, I'm all gitty. This is exciting to me. To think of Jake's expression when he sees what I come home with. Beth is a nut but she's usually right. I have five bags and a burning hot credit card, I think it's time to head home.

Beth and I grab a frozen yogurt before we leave. I'm reminded of when Jake, Kayla and I went to the Crunchy Cone. I feel that moment in love.

"Hey Beth, be good to Jake tomorrow. You guys will be together at the Telegram. Keep your hands off! He's all mine."

"I think it will be great working with him. It's a great way to really get to know him. Don't worry; I don't touch anymore, except for Jim."

"Thanks for tonight Bethy. I can't wait to be at the Cape this time tomorrow. I think we all need a bit of an escape."

"I think we should get really drunk. We haven't done that since... forget it, sorry girl."

"It's okay. I know, since Northeastern before the attack. It's okay, I'm finally okay with it. It's in the past and it's over."

"I think I'm going to have to give that Jake a kiss for bringing my girl back to me."

"Oh, no you don't. Thanks for tonight. You had better come to the door with me to make sure everything is okay. I didn't see Jake's car outside so he mustn't be home yet. He'll freak if I don't check every nook and cranny to make sure it's safe."

"I got my piece! I got you covered girl."

I looked back at her and laughed. The thought of her packing makes me laugh; when she gets married she'll probably have it in her garter belt.

We walked in and the small living room was glowing with candles and soft music playing. Jake was lying on the couch in a ready position.

"Beth, I think the coast is clear."

"Go get him girl. He's waiting for you. Love you."

FELICIA & JAKE

I slipped into the bathroom and put on the slinky little thing Beth made me buy. When I came out, Jake was leaning over the back of the couch waiting for me to come out of the bedroom.

"Fuck Felicia, you are gorgeous. Your angels show right through. Come over here so I can touch you."

"Have you been drinking?"

"Jim and I never made it to the racquetball court, so yeah; he gave me a ride home. Let's not waste our breath talking about Jim; you're going to need all your breath for what I want to do."

"Yes Jake! Don't you dare stop!"

Another nightmare free night for Jake. I'm a little embarrassed after last night to look into his bright eyes though. WOW!

"Good Morning Angel."

"Good Morning to you. How did you sleep?"

"The best I ever have. You were unbelievable. I think I owe Beth a thank you."

"I think I owe Jim one too."

We both laughed and shook our heads remembering

our incredible night. Time to get to business though. Jake and Beth will be going to The Telegram today to question a few people. Hoping to gain some insight on Amanda Styles and Frank Monroe's whereabouts. I'll be dropping Jake off at the bar he left his car at last night and going to the office. Praying there are no more kids coming forward.

"Have a great day Jake, I love you."

"You too Felicia. God I love you so much."

He kissed me and got into his car. Driving away from him, I immediately got a chill and a bad feeling. Where is this coming from? Something in my gut is telling me something is not right. I sure hope Amanda Styles is okay.

Trying to focus my mind on last night and not the feeling I have, I manage to smile. Erin greets me at the door and says that there is someone waiting for me in my office. She didn't get his name as he refused to give it.

FELICIA & FRANK

I walked in to my office and saw a man with brown hair and he stood up and shook my hand, not introducing myself to him. I was a bit nervous to shut the door but he motioned his arm for me to close it. I did.

"Felicia, I'm Frank Monroe. I don't want any harm."

"Well that's a relief Mr. Monroe. What can I do for you?"

"I'd like to report an assault. A sexual assault."

"I see, is this in regards to a foster child?"

"No."

"If it's not you should report it to the police."

"I can't.

"Why is that Mr. Monroe?"

"The one that was assaulted was me. The one who assaulted me was my cousin Harold Monroe."

"Mr. Monroe, I'm so sorry. I'm not sure why you aren't going to the police though."

"Captain Murphy is covering things up because my cousin paid his gambling debt. If I go to him he'll get the information to him and my family and I will be in danger."

"Don't worry; I think we can go to the District Attorney. That's whose handling all the cases. When did this happen to you?"

"It happened when I was twelve years old until I was sixteen. The guy is sick, really fucking sick. He has been blackmailing me for twenty-two years. I threatened to tell and he gave me a few options. Dead. Dead. Or Dead. I had no choice but to keep quiet but I told him it would cost him. So he bought the newspaper for me and he pays me handsomely."

"So why now? Why come forward now?"

"Miss Westfield, I have two daughters and I couldn't imagine either one of them going through that. After seeing the article in my paper while on vacation, I knew I couldn't keep quiet anymore."

"Where is Amanda Styles?"

"She is safe. She is in an undisclosed location right now. After I saw the article, I had to contact her and tell her to go away. If Harold got out on bail he would come after all of us."

"Thank god. Does she know about your abuse? She didn't want to print the story because of you but I think her conscience got the best of her."

"She knows Harold is my cousin, she also knows he gives the paper a lot of money. She also has seen how controlling he can be. I'm sure it was fear driven but I'm glad she printed it; it's about time that Bastard and his pig of a wife get what they deserve. No, Amanda doesn't know about my abuse."

"If you'll excuse me for a minute, I have to make a couple of phone calls."

"I'll wait here. Thank you Miss Westfield."

I had to call Jake and Jim and tell them that Frank Monroe is sitting in my office. After talking to them, they are all on their way here.

"Thank you for waiting Mr. Monroe, can I get you some coffee?"

"No thank you. I don't think my nerves can handle it. Miss Westfield, my wife doesn't know. Nobody knows."

"I'm so sorry. I know this isn't easy but you did the right thing. Time doesn't matter, what matters is justice."

"The funny thing is I've never had money problems because he was paying me but I haven't enjoyed my life at all. Every day those images come back in my mind… every day. They don't leave because I have a nice home or I can buy my kids what they want. They never leave."

"I know Mr. Monroe. Perhaps now you can start to heal now that you have taken the burden of that secret away."

"I don't care about the money; I just want to be free of him."

"You seem like a good man."

"Thank you but I've always blamed myself. Why couldn't I stop it? Why did he choose me? My parents loved Harold. He was very convincing. They would have me stay at his house for weekends at a time when they would go out of town. I couldn't say anything. I had to go and take what was coming to me. I tried not to go but my parents said that Harold loved me; I was his favorite little cousin. Sick Bastard."

Jake, Beth and Jim all arrived at the same time. I was happy to see them; this was getting a little heavy.

"Jake, Jim and Beth, this is Frank Monroe."

"Frank, this is Investigator Jake Brown, Assistant District Attorney Jim Hughes and Investigator Beth Kramer."

"Well, Mr. Monroe it is nice to finally meet you. We've all been looking for you. What brings you here," Jim asked.

Frank Monroe told the three of them what he told me. He broke down. He realized if he had come forward years ago he could've prevented this from happening to all these other kids. It was heart wrenching to witness.

"Mr. Monroe, would you be willing to testify in court against your cousin," Jim asked.

"Mr. Hughes, I think it's the least I can do for these

kids," Frank replied.

"You're a good man Frank. With all the evidence we have it may not get to court. Having you as a witness is definitely in our favor," Jim said.

"Whatever I can do to keep these two behind bars, I'll do. I'm going to have to have a conversation with my wife and soon. She doesn't know that I was a victim too."

"Frank I need to ask, is Harold Monroe a dangerous man," Jake asked.

"Honestly, what he is, is a spoiled brat that was born with a silver spoon in his mouth. He has had everything handed to him. Then he inherited millions when my aunt and uncle died. He's not dangerous without money, he's a weak man. With money he can buy his way out of anything. Yes he is a dangerous man because of his money."

"I don't think he'll have a penny when we're done with him," Jim piped up.

They all talked about what the next step was and we concluded the meeting.

"Can you believe this? After I dropped you off Jake, I had the weirdest feeling something was going to happen but I thought it was bad. I had no idea who he was."

"Felicia, this is great. We're getting to the bottom of this and girl, these kids will get their justice," Beth said.

"There's one more thing that needs to be done. It's time I take a walk through Captain Patrick Murphy's door. He may still have his house but he's not going to have his job. It's time for this money trail of the Monroe's to end," Jim said.

"You go get him Mr. District Attorney. I like the sound of that. I'm taking the rest of the day off and going home to get ready for our trip," Beth advised.

"Bethy, that sounds great; I think I'll do the same," I said.

"Jim, I think I'll go with you to see my old friend at the station," said Jake.

"Let's head out Jake so the ladies can go through our underwear draw and pack our stuff, "Jim said laughing, but serious.

The mood was so light and we all laughed. We are all anxiously awaiting the departure out of town. As much as I love Jake, I do like that he lifted the "No going alone." I'd like to take these few moments I have before we leave to sit and reflect on life.

"Good Afternoon Miss. I'm Assistant District Attorney Jim Hughes and this is Investigator Jake Brown, we're here to see Captain Murphy."

"I'll let him know you're here. You can have a seat."

"Thank you."

Captain Murphy opened the large steel door and greeted Jim and I with a puzzling and concerned look.

"Mr. Hughes, Jake, come back to my office," Captain Murphy invited them.

The three of us men of law walk back to his office, down the mundane hallway. To think this man spent his career on the Police Force and then falters over money. It's hard to wrap my head around it.

"What can I help you gentlemen with," Captain Murphy asked quite nervously.

"Captain Patrick Murphy, you are under arrest for conspiracy, obstruction of justice and evidence tampering. You have the right to remain silent. Anything you say can and will be used against you in a Court of law. You have the right to an attorney. If you cannot afford an attorney, one will be provided for you. Do you understand the rights I have just read to you," Jim recited.

"I do," Captain Murphy stated.

JAKE

This is a moment I would like to forget. A man I had looked up to and held to the highest standards has succumbed to greed.

"That was a tough one Jim. I think he knew right away when he saw us. His time had come and there was nowhere to hide."

"Jake, I'm sure this was tough for you but it had to be done. Decisions and actions have consequences and I intend for all the players to pay for their crimes."

"I'm with you all the way. Should we head home to see if we have Speedos in our suitcases?"

"We better. We'll pick you and Felicia up in an hour."

Jim and I parted and drove home. The time is getting near. I can't wait to put the ring on her finger. To have her be all mine forever.

"Felicia, I'm home. Are you ready?"

My heart sinks, she isn't answering. I ran to the bedroom and thank God she was sleeping. I'll be happy to be away and not feel like we have to walk on eggshells. Felicia doesn't seem at all concerned for her safety; of course she doesn't know all that I know.

I can't stand to just watch her sleep right now; I have to be near her. I slide in next to her and rub her forehead. She starts to move and wake up. Before she can say a word my lips are on hers. My self-control is losing the battle but I told Felicia I would never fuck her and that means no quickies either. She deserves to be pampered and caressed each and every time.

"Hey sleepy head. It's time to get up. Jim and Beth will be here soon."

"Oh, it's that time already? I guess I slept longer than I thought. Everything is packed so we have time."

"Not enough time to savor you."

"Thanks for the note on my windshield, you're so sweet. You don't have to worry about me. I'm safe Jake but it was still sweet."

"Remind me what the note said, my brain was fried when I wrote it."

"It said, see you soon. Be safe with a heart."

"Oh yeah, I guess I do worry too much sometimes. It's all good now though."

What the fuck, I didn't put a note on her windshield. "See you soon," that can only be a message from one person. Shit.

"Are you okay Jake? You just got real pale all of a sudden?"

"I'm fine. I just thought about Captain Murphy and how I looked up to him years ago and now he's going to prison."

"I know it's hard when someone you respect let's you down, but you did the right thing. This whole case is coming to an end and we'll be able to focus on happy things. Let's make this weekend about you and me, no shop talk okay?"

"Sounds perfect and exactly what I had in mind. You always make things better, I love you."

"I love you too Jake and I plan to show you how much this weekend."

I plan to show her how much I love her and treasure her. The door just got banged on, time to go. We packed up Jim's SUV and the girl's sat in the back as girly as they could be. That note is on the forefront of my mind. I need to talk to Jim about this. I know no shop talk this weekend but this will have to be in private.

Beth and I are playing the license plate game and punch buggy and she has a good right hook. It's like old times hanging out going on a road trip with her.

"Bethy where did you book our rooms? I can't believe I never asked you."

"The Chatham Bars Inn Resort and Spa, it's beautiful and we can have a massage and mani- pedis."

"It sounds perfect. I'm so glad we're doing this Beth. With everything going on and you guys buying a house and probably getting married soon, it's great that we can do this. Jim and Jake seem to have a lot in common and get along great, so that's a bonus."

"Me too. It's been way too long without my girl living. You're back to your old self. In fact, I think happier and more confident than ever before. No, Jim and I aren't getting married; we'll be broke after we buy the house. Jim thinks Jake is great; it's as if he has a new best friend."

"If it wasn't for you Bethy, I'd never had the nerve to talk to Jake. Well, I didn't have a choice in that but I never would have had the balls to ask him to my place. I owe you big time. Thanks for making me take a risk."

"Anytime girl. You two are meant to be and I don't think it was an accident that you two were working on the same case, just saying."

"What does that mean?"

"I believe in fate. I think it was fate how you two met and fell instantly in love. I told you once he laid eyes on you he would be smitten."

"I believe in fate too and that's what I told him. I'm so happy Bethy; I never thought I would ever be. I know I'll always be happy with Jake."

"I think you're right. I don't think anything could keep you two apart."

"What are you ladies talking about back there? It

sounds mushy," Jim asked.

"Nothing, just girl talk," Beth replied.

"I hope you're not telling our secrets Beth," Jim laughed.

"Too late for that Jim. You know I tell Felicia everything and I mean everything," Beth said with emphasis.

We all laughed. Up ahead is our exit. This ride went flying by. I can't wait to walk on the beach with Jake hand and hand. As we took the exit off the highway and drove toward the resort, I got that feeling back in my gut. What the hell is this all about? Everything is perfect, so why do I keep getting this pit in my stomach?

"We're here, this is so beautiful Felicia. This is exactly what you always used to say you wanted to do. I picked this place just for you my bestie!"

"Beth, it is absolutely breathtaking. It's almost identical to what I always used to daydream about when we would think about things we always wanted to do. You're so good to me."

We all got out of the SUV, grabbed our bags and went to check in. Beth got us each our own suites. Jake paid for our suite with his credit card which was a good thing because I just noticed I forgot mine.

"Are we getting together for dinner tonight Beth?"

Jim and Jake shared a look and Jim said, "Tonight will be our night to be alone in our fantasy suite."

"Jim, I didn't realize you watched the Bachelor. That sounds great to me," Jake said smiling, knowing this was what he hoped.

FELICIA

I looked over at Jake and he had a grin on his face that made me want to smother myself in him. We went up to the third floor where the suites were. Beth and Jim's was two doors down from ours. That was a good thing, not so sure I wanted to hear her and Jim all night.

Jake opened the door and the room was magnificent. There were fresh flowers surrounding the living area. Glass French Doors looked out to the Atlantic Ocean. There was an ice bucket with a bottle of champagne filling it. The bedroom was painted in a soft pink; with a canopy and the bed was positioned facing the ocean.

"Felicia do you like it?"

"Jake, like isn't a strong enough word. I love it, this is beyond beautiful. I could spend the rest of my life here with you."

"That sounds good but we are actually taking a ride on a boat to a private beach in thirty minutes."

"That sounds lovely and romantic. Can I unpack and change my clothes before we leave?"

"If you make it quick. I don't want anyone stealing our boat. I want it to be just you and me."

"I like the sounds of that. I'll be quick and ready, don't you worry."

I went inside the bedroom and quickly put our clothes in the dresser. With all that Beth made me buy, I don't think I'll need more than one draw because everything is tiny. I put on my new pale yellow sundress and put my hair up in a high ponytail. I walked out to the living area and Jake had a pair of navy blue flat front pair of shorts on with a white shirt with a navy stripe. He was handsome, sexy and all mine.

"You look stunning Angel. Your halo is making a small appearance in that dress. Very sexy. I see the boat coming up, we better get down there."

JAKE

I grabbed her hand and we hurried down to the dock to be taken to the private beach. I have everything we need, blanket, champagne, the ring and by far the most beautiful girl I've ever seen.

We got on the boat; it was a small motor boat, a

shuttle on the water. Felicia and I sat on the right side edge admiring the view. My stomach is in knots, I must admit. I'm nervous and excited at the same time. Felicia is quiet. I'm not sure why. I just want this to be perfect for her. I want it to be like one of her daydreams that she would have with Beth. The boat is coming to a stop and we jumped off onto another dock that lead us directly to a private beach surrounded by water. Our own little island for the time being. I paid a pretty penny for the boat not to bring anyone out here for three hours.

"Jake, this is unbelievable. Are we all alone here?"

"Yes Angel, it's just you and me for the next three hours."

"Thank you. This is like a dream come true."

"It sure is. Is everything okay Felicia?"

"Yes of course, how couldn't it be?"

"You seem a bit quiet."

"It's nothing. I don't want to ruin this beautiful evening."

"Tell me what's on your mind Angel, I can tell something is bother you, I'm here for you for the good and bad."

"Have you ever had a bad feeling in your gut? When

you don't know what it is but something isn't right?"

"Yes, is that what's bugging you?"

"Yeah, I got it earlier today too and then Mr. Monroe was sitting in my office."

"That was a good thing though, maybe the feeling you have is a good thing."

"You're probably right. I think the last two weeks have just caught up to me you know?"

"I do know, but this weekend is our time. We're not going to think about anything bad, sad or work related. Let's just think about you and me, okay?"

"You always seem to know how to make me feel better. Let's think of you and me, that's an easy plan."

Jake placed the blanket on the sand and we sat down, burying our feet in the sand. Then his lips were upon mine. Within seconds, the heat and passion were scalding and his hands began to wander.

"It's just you and me Angel, lay back and relax. Let me submerge myself in your body. Let me please you."

He slowly pulls down the strap of my sundress and lathered his tongue and lips over my shoulder and over my neck. Shivers are enveloping me. He pulls the other strap down and does the same. He then exposes my breasts and his heated mouth took hold of my nipple and my hips begin to buck at the sensation. With his thumb, he clasps the other nipple and lightly elongates it causing my inner core to tingle. His breathing is matching mine, heavy and pant-like.

With his manly fingers, he is trailing the outline of my breast and his eyes are leaking a teardrop. His mouth follows a path to my belly button and he licks all around it. His tongue and mouth are eager to go further down. He grabs my hand and holds it as he places light kisses between my thighs and stops on my pulsating nub.

"Look at me Felicia; I want to see how this makes you feel.'"

I looked down at him as he is in my intimate spot and I can't speak. His tongue is magical. He added a finger and he was taking me over the edge. My hips thrust up against his mouth and I crumble in the wake of this earth shattering orgasm.

He pushed his hardness into me, slow and gentle movements as we found our perfect rhythm. He stares into my eyes as our bodies are one and he never looks away. My love for him is infinite. Our bodies are matching each other's and I could feel him swell as another orgasm creeps up and tightens around him and we explode together.

The waves are crashing in the background and sand is lathering our feet. It feel impossible for this to be real and not a dream.

"Jake, I love you. I love making love with you. Here with you on this private beach is dreamlike."

"Angel, I want to make love to you forever. Our bodies fit perfectly together. If I could freeze this moment in time I would. Every time we make love I feel like it's a dream. "

"How about a swim in that beautiful ocean in front of us Bright Eyes?"

"I could certainly use a cooling off."

We walked the few feet to the water and jumped the waves. I floated in his arms as he lifted me over the crests. His wet, hard body made me want him again. We swam around a bit and wanted to take advantage of walking on the beach alone together.

He went back to the blanket and got me a towel to wrap around me. We walked hand and hand, admiring every bit of nature around us. Jake picked up a shell and turned his back to me for a moment.

When he turned back to me and his face was serious. His eyes gleaming an aqua color; he just stared at me and grabbed my left hand. With my hand in his, he crouched down in the sand got on one knee and it began.

"Felicia Westfield, from that first moment I saw you, nameless and unknown to me, I knew that I had to meet you. When I walked into Dr. Sandy's office that day, selfishly, I was only thinking of kissing your lips. My body and mind went into a place it had never entered. I just knew from that first look in your eyes you were the other part of me. You were my soul mate. You have taught me so much in a short time and you have made me feel like I finally found home. Everything about you is perfect and magical to me. I want to spend every day of my life making you happy and loved. I want to have all my firsts with you and give you everything you always deserved but never felt or had. Felicia Westfield, will you marry me?"

He opened up the shell and the ring gleamed at me. It is the most beautiful ring I have ever seen. I'm not just saying it either. I hesitated for a moment and began.

"Jake Brown, you changed my life the moment I saw you. You gave me life again. You revived my body, my senses and my mind. You have made me feel secure with my scarred and damaged body. You are comfort to me. There is nothing more than I want for my life is to spend every day going to bed and waking up next to you. I love you more than I could ever explain. I want to make you happy and secure all the days forward. Yes, I will marry you."

He put the ring on my left hand and pulled me in for a hug. I have no doubt, wherever we are together, I have found home.

"You scared me Angel, with that hesitation. I thought you were going to reject me."

Finding Home

"You can't reject part of yourself Jake, we are one."

"Is it possible to love you even more in this moment?"

"I seem to be asking myself the same question."

He held my now ringed hand and walked me back to the blanket and opened the champagne.

"To my future wife and I hope it's the very near future. To a life of no more past and only the present and our future together. To the most kindhearted, compassionate, sexy, beautiful woman I am proud to call my wife. Cheers."

"To us, you and me Jake. To no more scars, no more fears and to our long and amazing life together. You are my forever and my always. One more thing… to Fate and Love at First Sight! Cheers."

We kissed as it was our first kiss and sparks went off. This was the best day of my life. No more bad feelings in my gut, there's no room for it with all the love I feel. This must have been what it was.

We heard the motor of the boat coming to bring us back to shore. We got our things together and went Back to the dock to get on the boat. We sat in silence as we had on the way here but this time it was a jubilant silence with his hand in mine rubbing the ring that symbolizes so much.

We got back to the resort, Jake went to the front desk to ask about something and I went up the suite. There was a note on our door.

"See you soon, hope you're having fun."

Beth, she's always doing weirdo stuff like that. The note made me smile. I couldn't be happier. I took off my wet bathing suit and ran and turned on the shower. I heard the door open and smiled knowing Jake would be joining me. A few minutes went by and he hadn't come in yet. I heard footsteps and his breathing and he pulled back the curtain exposing his beautiful maple leaf.

"Is there room for two in here?"

"I don't know. You may have to get real close to me."

"Felicia, you are so damn sexy. I can't get enough of you."

"Then have me."

So it began again, each touch is more amazing than the next. After our shower and incredible love making, I had to text Beth. This ring on my finger is glaring so bright and I have to tell her.

I got my phone out and texted her:

"Bethy, are you busy? I have talk to you."

A few minutes passed and my phone sang a song, she texted me back.

"Felicia, I have to talk to you too. Why don't we send the boys to the bar and you come to my suite."

"Sounds perfect. I'll be there in a few minutes."

JAKE & JIM

As much as I wanted to be with Felicia every second tonight, I had to talk to Jim alone and this was perfect. I had to find out about David. The note on Felicia's car before we left hasn't left my mind.

"Hey Jim, how'd it go? Did she say yes?"

"It was unbelievable. She had no clue. Of course she said yes, wouldn't you?"

"I suppose if I was into guys, yeah."

We both laughed and I asked him how it went with Beth and he said perfect.

"I hate to bring up the subject but I'm glad we got to break out on our own. What have you heard about David's parole," Jake asked.

"Nothing since the last time we talked about it. Why what's up?"

"Felicia got a note on her car that said, "See you soon. "This is what David said to her at the prison. Could it be him?"

"Not personally, he's still in prison but he could be having someone else doing it perhaps."

"Do you think he'll come after her when he gets out?"

"I think he'd be pretty stupid if he did. He'd be right back in prison if he did. Maybe it isn't even related to him?"

"I have a bad feeling man. Right now she thinks it was from me. I played it off as it was; I hate not telling her about his parole. It's killing me but it's the best thing to do."

"When we get back I'll check on things and see what I can find out."

"That's all I can ask. So, did Beth say when she wanted the wedding?"

"She said she didn't want to wait and wanted a small wedding."

"Did you tell her that I was proposing?"

"No way! I couldn't take that away from Felicia. She would want to tell her. These two are like two peas in a pod."

"I can see that."

FELICIA & BETH

I walked to Beth's room just staring at the ring on my finger shining from the lights in the hallway. I knocked and she opened the door with her newly lit up left hand ring finger.

"Oh my god Bethy, congratulations. Tell me everything."

I tried to keep my hand behind my back not to spoil this moment for her. She told me how Jim ordered them dinner by room service. He had a bouquet of pink roses delivered up with the food. While they were eating, he was being all sappy and emotional. When she took her third bite of her crab cake there was something hard inside that almost broker her tooth. It was a ring.

Beth was so excited and she cried telling me. She doesn't cry often. To see her this happy makes me even happier. After a bunch of going nowhere boyfriends, she finally found her man.

"Felicia, I don't want to wait to get married. I want to be Mrs. Hughes so bad. I just can't believe this is happening. I had no idea. I love him so much and he really loves me. Funny huh?"

"It's not funny, it's fantastic and you deserve this so

much. You two are meant to be together. He's a lucky guy and cute."

"We had the most incredible sex after. I honestly thought I was going to come like guys do."

"Spare me the details Bethy."

"What did you and Jake do?"

"He rented some time on the private beach for a few hours. We hung out and swam, drank champagne, it was awesome."

"Please tell me you had Sex on the Beach."

"Mind blowing fucking sex."

"There you go again with the F-bomb— loving it. It's crazy when you think about the two of us, finally finding love."

"I think I'm beginning to like the F-bomb, it makes things mean more. I'd say we're pretty lucky Bethy."

We both laughed. Beth went and opened the mini bar and poured us a drink to celebrate. When I grabbed the glass, I forgot about the ring.

"Felicia Fucking Westfield, what is that on your finger? Why didn't you tell me?"

"I didn't want to ruin your moment. You and Jim have

been together a lot longer than Jake and I and you deserved the glory."

"It's stunning Felicia. I'm over the moon happy for you. When are you going to get married?"

"I don't know but I don't want to wait. I see no reason to wait."

"This is perfect. Let's get married together, a duel wedding!"

"Really? You would want that? I'd love that."

"Yes! We are doing it. It'll be so awesome and we can go on our honeymoon together too."

My stomach is tingling with excitement. Beth is like the only family I have. Our weddings will be shared and I wouldn't want it any other way. If it wasn't for Beth I'd still be existing in a colorless world.

"Thanks Bethy for the note you left on my door, you're so cute."

"What note? I didn't write you a note. I wish I had thought about it but I had better things on my mind if you know what I mean?"

"You really didn't? Than who would have left me a note? It wasn't Jake because he was with me?"

"Maybe someone put it on the wrong door."

"I never thought of that, you're probably right."

Just then, the door opened and the men came in. Each one congratulating us. We told them about our plan for a duel wedding just as Jim had figured. They were on board. The four of us sat on the deck looking out at the ocean having a drink and planning our weddings. We laughed, joked, and had too much to drink into the wee hours of the night.

Jake and I left Jim and Beth as Beth was getting pretty frisky with Jim. We went back to our suite and crawled in to bed. Jake snuggled in behind me with his arms wrapped around me and we fell fast asleep.

JAKE & FELICIA

I woke up in a cold sweat and I was trembling. Jake woke up as well.

"Felicia, what is it?"

"I had a nightmare. It seemed so real Jake."

"What was it about?"

"David. He got out of jail and came after me. I haven't had that dream since we've been together. I'm sorry I woke you up."

"Come here Angel. David will never hurt you again. It's a nightmare, that's all it is. I'll never let anyone hurt you again."

"You're right, it's just a nightmare. David can't hurt me. It's just so weird that I had it after not having it for a while. I don't know why that was in my mind after our beautiful day today. It came out of the blue. Jake, I need you. I need to feel safe."

"I'm right here. I'll always be here."

"Please make love to me Bright Eyes. I need to feel you; I need that connection right now."

We made love and I began to feel better. I hate that dream. It's always the same. We fell back asleep and without any more interruptions, we slept until eight o'clock.

The ocean was calm it must be low tide. I sat on the deck and watched the waves come in and the tide go out. I was mesmerized by the possibilities that the ocean offered. Jake came from behind and handed me a cup of coffee, which I desperately needed. He joined me in watching the waves and it was another moment that I would cherish.

Today we went shopping and laid on the beach. We even attempted to play beach volleyball but Beth and I couldn't keep up, so we went back to the blanket and got some more rays.

"Hey Beth, thanks for making all the arrangements to come here. I'll never forget this trip. It's so calming and refreshing here," I said hugging her.

"My pleasure girl. I'll never forget it either. I'm so glad we can add this to our real daydreams," Beth said still hugging me.

We both laughed and chatted about some of our old time memories. It was great to just be, not having to worry about more abused kids coming in nor Harold Monroe or anyone else.

After way too many hours in the sun we all walked up to our suites and got ready for dinner. The four of us ate an amazing dinner and then went to the outdoor bar where there was live entertainment. Jake danced with me and held me close to him whispering luscious things in my ear. Jim and Beth danced and it felt like a rehearsal for our weddings.

It was a terrific night and it's only going to get better when we get behind closed doors. The toys are coming out. Jake and I went back to our suite and that's when he saw the note from the night before.

"Felicia, where did this note come from," Jake asked.

"It was taped to the door last night. I thought Beth put it there but she said no. It was probably put on the wrong door."

His demeanor changed that instant. He kept putting his hands through his hair. He began to pace. He was making me nervous.

"Jake, what's the matter? It's only a note."

"I'm fine. I was just thinking about another man wanting you and touching you."

"Don't be silly. You're the only one for me. Come here and let me show you."

We had wild and hot sex for hours. It seemed to take Jake's mind off what was bugging him. We fell asleep naked, wrapped up in each other and we both slept through the night without nightmares.

In the morning we went for breakfast and to the beach for a couple hours before driving back home. This weekend was complete bliss but it's always good to go home especially now that I have found home.

JAKE

The ride home was stop and go for a while with the traffic. Beth and I fell asleep in the back seat. When Jim turned into the parking lot of Jake's place, I got that gut feeling again. Shit what the hell is wrong?

"Jim, Beth, we had an amazing time this weekend.
Let's make this an annual trip," Jake said.

"Sounds good Jake. I'll call you tomorrow," Jim said.

Felicia and I got out of the car and walked up to the
door. The door was unlocked. I know damn well it
was locked when we left.

"Felicia, call Beth and Jim and tell them to turn
around. I don't want you waiting outside by yourself."

"What's going on Jake?"

"The door is unlocked and I have to check things out
before you come in."

Beth and Jim turned the corner and Jim got out of the
car to go in with Jake. Beth and I stayed in the car
holding hands.

Jim and I walked in the door, at first glance everything
looked intact. We both walked in the bedroom and
that's where it was. Spray-painted over the bed:

"This is NOT over. See You Soon."

"What the fuck Jim? She can't come in here and see
this. It's David, it has to be."

"Jake, it might not be David. You and Felicia have a

few people upset about being exposed. Let's call this in and see if they can find some prints."

"This is fucked up. Can you follow us to her place after and see if anything is wrong there? She'll be getting a gun; I'll take her to the range today. I have to keep her safe Jim."

"You're both going to be fine. I'll have some protection for her and you for that matter. We don't know who this is intended for."

"I know its David. He said the same words at the prison. I can't let anything happen to her, I'll never forgive myself."

Beth and Felicia got outside of the car when they saw the police. I met them outside so they wouldn't come in. I held Felicia close to me while the police went inside and talked with Jim.

"What's going on Jake," I asked.

"It looks like someone broke in. I'm sure it was just some punk. Everything will be fine Felicia," he said unconvincingly.

"Whoever did it probably saw us leaving with our bags and figured it was a free for all. Let's go stay at my place tonight." I said, grabbing his hand and leading him to the car.

"We can do that but we are going to the shooting

range first. You're going to learn to fire a gun. I can't take any chances," Jake is now demanding.

"Jake, for god's sakes! Just because someone broke in doesn't mean I have to carry a lethal weapon," I snarled.

"Felicia, this is Beth talking to you, I carry one and you know that. In this day and time you have to protect yourself, get the goddamn gun."

"Beth, what is this, a fucking conspiracy? I don't like guns. I don't want to carry a gun and I don't want to fire a gun."

"Angel please, for me?

"Jake, I really am uncomfortable with it. Beth, do you really think I should?"

"Just do it Felicia, it's kind of cool too. It's powerful. You'll hopefully and probably never have to use it but having it in the rare instance if you need it, it's peace of mind," Beth insisted.

"Fine! Damnit! But I'm not happy about it. If you two will shut up about it I'll do it."

Jake kissed me on the cheek and thanked me. What the hell is the problem? I don't get why the heck I have to carry a frieken gun. I'll probably shoot my foot off. Beth is just as adamant as Jake is. It's pissing me off.

Jim and Beth stayed with the police and Jake took me to the shooting range. He got me all set up, wrapping his arms around me to position the barrel. Headphones on, target in place, finger on trigger. I shut my eyes and pulled the trigger. My entire body shook. I hit the target. It was actually exhilarating. We shot for about an hour and then went to the gun store and applied for a license. Maybe it won't be that bad. I did feel powerful. I still liked the mace route though.

"Jake, what has you so freaked out? You seem like you are very anxious. What are you not telling me?"

"Felicia, I just wouldn't be able to live with myself if something happened to you. With everything that has happened with the Monroes and then going to the prison, it reminds me of how many bad people are out there. I just want you to be safe it I'm not with you. I love you Angel."

"I love you too Jake but please know I'm not that comfortable with this. However, it did kind of feel good to shoot. It was a rush."

FELICIA

Jake is still upset about the break in. He's such a manly man. It surprises me that he is so uptight. They didn't take anything, just messed a few things up he said. The bizarre thing is why am I not freaking out? I lived the last three and half years in fear and now, it's as if I'm immune to it. I'll take it though; I lived too long looking over my shoulder not living.

Before we got to my apartment, Jake called the police to escort us in to make sure nobody was inside. He is losing it. I asked him about it and he gave me the same answer, "I just need to make sure you're safe." I like that he wants to protect me but there has to be something more to this, something he isn't telling me.

We pulled into a parking spot at my complex and the police were there waiting. Jake got out of the car and had me stay outside with an officer. The cop and Jake went inside, checked every nook and cranny and were given the all clear. He thanked the cops and I was now allowed in.

"Jake, you're making me start to get paranoid. Are you not telling me something?"

"I'm sorry Angel; I think my mind is on overdrive. I'm not keeping anything from you. I wouldn't do that. Can we just get changed and go lay in bed? I just want to hold you. Can we do that?"

"That sounds perfect. I just want to hold my fiancé too. Everything is okay Jake; please put those worried eyes away. I'm with you; I'll always be with you."

JAKE

What the fuck, this is making me crazy. I'm making her doubt me and be paranoid. I have to get a hold of myself. I pray Jim finds out tomorrow about David. I have to sleep; maybe it will stop my mind. I spoon her from behind. There is no sex, just closeness and that's what I need. To feel her near me. She smells so good, that sweet pea smell. She is my home.

FELICIA

Monday morning, I roll over to find the space beside me empty again. I smell coffee brewing which is a god sent along with the man who has made it. I'm engaged. It's sinking in. This weekend was like a fantasy until we got home. I lay in the bed twirling this beautiful gem on my finger and I decide I can't wait to marry him. Beth and Jim are moving this weekend; the following weekend will be perfect.

Dress shopping, I never thought I would ever do that. I wish my mother were here to help me pick one out or give me her advice. I miss her so much even after this long. My heart sinks; I realize I have no one to walk me down the aisle. The only people I have in my life are Jake, of course, Beth, Jim and the Bishop kids. No family or relatives. Ouch, that hurts when I take inventory like that.

"Hey Angel, good morning to you. What are you thinking about in that beautiful head of yours?"

"Good Morning Bright Eyes. I was just hit by a realization I have no family, nobody to walk me down the aisle to become your wife."

"You have the family I have, each other. That's all we need. I'd like to see you walk down the aisle alone so there's nothing or nobody that will distract my eyes from the angelic woman walking to become my wife."

"Jake, what did I do to deserve you? You're right, we are family and that's all I need. I want to get married the week after next. What do you think?"

"Really? I even think that is too long but I'll wait until then. I'd marry you today but I would never take this day from you and Beth."

"If we keep talking about this Jake, we'll never get to work and I will ravage you with slow, deep love making."

His boxers immediately became a tent. This man makes me throb in all the right places. There's no time unfortunately to have my wish. The fantasy is over and it's back to work.

Jake dropped me off at work. He has some work with Jim to take care of today. I can't imagine what I'm facing when I walk in my office. I'm hoping for monotony. I completely forgot to call Beth this morning; I had better call her now before she starts freaking out too.

I walked in my office, before I started my day; I rummaged through my purse to find my phone. Finally, after clearing out receipts and used tissues I found it. I had a text. I'm not recognizing the phone number. The text reads:

"You think you have it all Felicia Westfield. You'll have nothing but an end. See you soon!"

I reread the message about five times and my hands were a shaky mess. I tried to call Jake but there was no answer. My entire body trembling, I dial Beth's number.

FELICIA & BETH

"Hey girly, you're late calling."

"Sorry Beth."

"What's wrong Felicia, you sound upset?"

"Beth, I have a text from someone and I don't know who it's from. Remember the note I thought you left on my suite door? I had gotten one on my car windshield before we left for the Cape and it said, ***"See you soon."***

"Who do you think it could be? Did you tell Jake?"

"He knows about the other notes. I thought the first one was from him and he acted like it was. He didn't answer his phone; he's supposed to be at Jim's office. Beth, does someone want to hurt me?"

"Felicia, nobody is going to hurt you. Someone's just probably playing a joke on you or something. You have to get your gun today though; it'll make you feel better just in case."

"That's helpful Beth, 'just in case.' I've had a reoccurring bad feeling and each time I've had it something good has happened. Now, I know this feeling I have is not good."

"I'll tell you what, I'm going to call Jim and let him know about this and tells him to have Jake call you. You sit tight okay?"

"Okay, I'm staying in my office."

BETH & JIM

Holy shit, is David after her? She has no idea that he may be getting out on parole. That motherfucker if he goes near her, I'll shoot him in the ball sack myself.

"Hey Jim, is Jake with you?"

"Hey baby, he was supposed to be here but he hasn't gotten here yet. What's up?"

I told Jim about the text Felicia got and the other two

notes. He told me that David wasn't getting out on parole for at least another month. He didn't think it was him.

"Jim, he's not answering his phone. Felicia is freaking out. What do we do? I can't have anything happen to my best friend. She's been through enough to last her a lifetime."

"I know baby. Everything will be fine, I promise you."

"Could this be coming from Harold Monroe?"

"It could be but I don't think so. I'll need the phone number that call came from so I can trace it."

"I'll call Felicia back and get it and let her know Jake's not there yet."

Shit, I don't want to call her back; I don't want to scare her even more that Jake isn't at Jim's office yet. I dial her number in hopes he called her back by now.

BETH & FELICIA

"Hey girl, I just talked to Jim and he said Jake isn't there yet. He probably stopped for coffee or something."

"Beth, he already had his coffee this morning and he very rarely has more than that until later in the day. Something's not right. Beth, I just found home with him, I can't lose him."

"Felicia, he's okay. He is capable of taking care of himself. Don't let your mind take over. I'm sure he just stopped somewhere on the way."

"I wish he had the damn IPhone than I could track it. I think I'm going to be sick Beth."

"You're going to be fine. Take a deep breath and think realistically. He will be at Jim's shortly. Before I forget, Jim wants the phone number that the text came from. He will trace it to see who it belongs to.

"Great, I forgot he could do all those things."

I gave Beth the phone number. It's the same area code as me at least that could help narrow it down a tad. I called Jake's number again, no answer. I leave him a desperate message. I don't know what to do.

FELICIA & ERIN

Erin knocked on my office door and I jumped.

"Felicia, are you okay? You look like you've been crying? Holy Crap, look at that rock on your finger," Erin shrieked.

"Hey Erin, I'm okay. Has Jake called in at all?"

"No, but this letter came for him. So you got engaged, tell me the details," Erin said all girly.

"Erin, it's not a good time but yes we got engaged."

"If anyone was going to snag that beautiful man up I'm glad it was you. Are you sure you're okay," Erin asked.

"No, but I will be when I hear from Jake. Has anyone else come in to report abuse from the Monroes?"

"Not since you left on Friday, thankfully. That guy is a sicko for sure," Erin said cringing her nose.

"He sure is. I'm so glad he's finally locked up. I'll tell you all about the engagement in a little while; I have to get to work."

"I'll be in my office. If you decide to tell me what's wrong, I'll still be in my office," Erin said walking out.

Erin left my office. This letter is burning a hole in my hand. This is so unlike me but under the circumstances, I have to open it.

Dear Jake:

It was so good of you to come see me after three years. You still think you're going to end up making something of yourself. Fat chance son, you are made of me. That pretty little pussy you have will be crying out after you beat her. You can't run and hide from Biology. It's in you Jake. Don't kid yourself. I am inside of your mind and I'll never leave.

I have a good friend in here. He says to say hello to Felicia for him. He's not too happy about your engagement; he says that she belongs to him. I'd better watch your step son if I were you. You should never steal someone's pussy.

See you soon,
Dad

JIM & FELICIA

Thank god, the cleaning crew empties the barrel because I just filled it up with vomit. David. Where is Jake? I picked up my phone and dialed Jake's number again. Still no answer. Then I dialed Jim's number.

"Jim Hughes speaking."

"Jim, its Felicia. Is Jake there yet?"

"Not yet, I expect him shortly. I looked into the phone number and it is a prepaid cell phone. I can't track it, I'm so sorry. Are you okay?"

"Jim, I'm not okay. I just opened a letter from Jake's dad from prison. He knows David. He knows about our engagement."

"Listen to me Felicia, they are both in prison and they can't hurt you. Let's try to remain calm and I will find out what's going on. I'm calling Beth to have her come pick you up and bring you to my office."

"Thank you Jim."

BETH & FELICIA

While I sit and wait for Beth to come retrieve me, I feel like a puppy that can't go out yet on her own. My phone buzzed. Please be from Jake. I look down and it was the same number the last text came from:

"Loving the Maple Leaf. Nice Try."

Someone has Jake. I can't breathe. What could anyone want to hurt him for; he's the nicest man I've ever met.

"Beth, thank god you're here. Do you have your piece?"

"Girl, calm down, yes I have my piece."

We hurried down the stairs to get to the car. As we are driving to Jim's office, I tell Beth about the letter and the new text. She seems nervous now. That's never good. She doesn't frazzle easy. We are a few blocks from the District Attorney's office and I see a car that looks like Jake's.

"Turn around Beth! I think I just saw Jake's car on the side of the road. Oh my god, he has to be okay."

"He's fine Felicia. Please don't think the worst."

She turned around and we pulled up right behind the car. It was in fact Jake's car. Beth pulled her gun out and had it ready. We both walked up to the car and noticed he had a flat tire and his hazards were on but the car was empty. There was an office park on the street that the car was pulled over on. Beth and I went inside to see if they saw anyone get out of the car or something else.

The first office we went to was of no help. We went to all the offices on the first floor in this building and nothing. We went up to the second floor and asked the woman at the front desk if we could speak to the people that have the offices in the front of the building.

A man and a woman came out and we asked them both if they had seen anyone in regards to the car in the breakdown lane with the hazard lights on. The man spoke up:

"When I was coming in, I saw a tall guy get out of his car and look at his tires. Before I got into the building the police showed up behind him so I figured he was all set. When I got to my office, I saw the officer cuff him and put him in the back seat of the cruiser."

"Thank you very much sir. What was your name?"

"Brad Turner."

"Can you tell us anything about the officer that was there and did he have a partner with him?"

"He was on the shorter side, much shorter
than the other guy. There was someone in the back
seat but I didn't get a good look. That's about all I got.
I figured he was being arrested for something."

"Thank you very much for your time sir. Have a good
day."

What could Jake have done that would get him
arrested? At least we know he's at the police station.
Beth got on the phone and called Jim to tell him. Jim
was meeting us at the police station but told us not to
go in without him.

Beth and I were waiting in the parking lot of the
station. My palms were like a melted Popsicle. Beth
kept looking out the window all around us. Finally, we
saw Jim pull up. We got out of the car to meet him to
walk in together.

JIM

"Hello, I'm ADA Jim Hughes; I would like to see
someone that has been brought in within the last hour
or so. His name is Jake Brown."

"Let me take a look to see who's been brought in. I'm
sorry sir, but there's no Jake Brown. There's only been
one person brought in today and it was a woman. Is
there anything else I can help you with?"

"Yes, when was that woman brought in and can you get me the Chief."

"Just one minute sir, I'll try his office. She was brought in at 6:17 am for prostitution."

"Thank you."

Beth and I are holding hands. She's trying to hold me up. Something is wrong here. Jim looks over his shoulder at us and tries to be reassuring with his expression.

"Mr. Hughes, Chief Marrin says to go on back to his office. It's right down the hall, third door on the left. The women have to stay out here though."

"Thank you. Beth, keep her calm. We'll figure this all out and get Jake back. Give me a few minutes with the chief."

Now sobbing, Felicia is getting more scared and yelled out, "Jim hurry! I know something is really wrong."

"I'll be back in a few. Have the lady get you both something to drink."

Walking down this hallway, my gut is telling me there's trouble. I knocked on the Chief's door and he called for me to come in.

JIM & THE CHIEF

"Hello Chief, Jim Hughes, Assistant District Attorney."

"Nice to meet you, Mr. Hughes. What can I help you with?"

"It seems a friend of mine was taken into custody on the side of the road by one of your officers. There's no record of him being booked or even brought in. I need to know every officer that is on the road and where they are."

"What are you suggesting Mr. Hughes? Are you thinking one of our officers kidnapped your friend?"

"It's possible. He's been working on the Monroe case and as you know Captain Murphy was arrested because he was being paid by Harold Monroe."

"Yes, quite a disgrace to this department. What is your friend's name?"

"Jake Brown."

"Jake, he was one of my students in the academy, nice man and turned out to be a great cop, wish he hadn't left the department. Let me call over to dispatch and see who's on the road and what cars are out. If one of my guys has him, we'll find him."

"We better make it fast Chief."

The chief was on the phone with dispatch for a while

and was writing faster than I could even think. He hung up the phone with a concerned look on his face.

"What is it Chief?"

"It's seems that Officer Mason is not answering, every other office is accounted for. Sally in dispatch is looking up where is car is on the map."

"A witness said there was someone else in the car as well. How long has this Officer Mason been on the force?"

"He just transferred over from Boston PD about a week ago."

"Interesting… can you call Sally back and see what she has found?"

As he was going to pick up the phone, his phone rang.

"Chief, it appears that Officer Mason's car is out of sector. Way out of sector. His patrol car is on Juniper Way. This is a camp ground," Sally told him.

"Thank you Sally, let me know if he moves."

"Will do sir."

"We have a location. I'm calling my men to respond to that location."

"I'm going with them. I have Jake's fiancé and my

fiancé out in the waiting area. They have to be protected."

"We'll take care of them, let's get you with Officer Bingham. We're going to get your friend back."

The Chief went out, talked with the girls and brought them back to his office so he could keep them abreast of what was going on. Felicia was a wreck as well as Beth and even myself. That name Mason sounds familiar. As I sit in the back of the cruiser like a criminal, hearing the shrieks of the sirens, I rack my brain to figure out why I know the name Mason. It comes to me; Harold Monroe's attorney's last name was Mason. Oh fuck, David's last name is Mason too. I never put two and two together at the arraignment.

"How much farther until we get there," Jim asked anxiously.

"About five more miles sir," said Officer Bingham.

"Make it quick, this could be ugly when we get there," Jim said.

"I'm doing my best without killing us all in the process," said Officer Bingham.

Felicia will be devastated if anything happens to Jake. We all will be. The sirens stop as we approach the road we need to turn on. It's a dirt road. It doesn't appear anyone is around. The five cruisers behind us pull down the road and we approach Officer Mason's cruiser in front of a small cabin. All the radios in the cruisers have been shut off so he couldn't hear if anyone was coming after him.

JIM, THE OFFICERS & MASON

The officers all got out of their cars with their weapons drawn and the building is surrounded. Officer Bingham, his partner and I go to the front door of the cabin and knock on the door.

"Mason, we know you're in there. Let's make this nice and easy and open up the door," Officer Bingham yelled out.

There's silence.

"Mason, this is your last chance! Open up or I'm breaking the door down," Officer Bingham now saying with force.

"Don't come any closer, if you do, they will both be dead," Mason yelled out like a crazy man.

One of the officers came around front and informed us there were three people in the cabin. Officer Mason, a man and a woman. The woman is tied up and bound and the man is cuffed and bound. Officer Mason has two guns, one facing each of them. The woman is tied to the bed and the man is tied to a chair.

"Mason, what do you want with these people? Nobody is worth ruining your career over. Let's talk this out," Officer Bingham changed his tone and tried to sound compassionate.

We hear some noises from inside and then a shot goes off.

"Mason, I hope you didn't just do what I think you did. You're not leaving us much choice, you are surrounded and there's no way out," Officer Bingham shouted out.

"I have a job to do and I'm not coming out until it's done. These two will pay for what they've done," Mason exclaimed.

Officer Jeffries comes around the front and says he has a clear shot at him. Mason is sitting in a chair facing the man and the woman. He wants to take the shot. I'm telling him to take the shot.

"Mason, this is Assistant District Attorney Hughes. This is your final chance to let the hostages out. We don't want anyone hurt."

"No fucking way am I letting these two out," Mason reiterated.

"Have it your way Mason. You've been warned," Jim called out.

I went around back to see if Officer Jeffries still had a

clear shot. I could see Jake and a woman and they both were alive. Mason was still sitting with a gun in each hand facing both hostages. He turned his head to the right, brought his gun up higher and closer to Jake and there was a shot. Mason is down. I wasn't sure who made the shot.

I ran around front to let Officer Bingham know it was clear, Mason was down. They broke down the door and we entered to find Jake bound and gagged and Amanda Styles from The Telegram tied up to the bed with half of her clothes on. We untied them and covered Miss Styles up.

"Took you long enough Jim. I thought I was going to bite the dust here. Where's Felicia? Is she okay?"

"Hey man, I waited for you at my office; I figured you were always late like Felicia. The girls saw your car on the side of the road. I got here as soon as we could pinpoint where the cruiser was. Felicia is fine, scared out of her mind, but fine. She's at the Station with Chief Marrin," Jim conveyed.

"Can I use your phone Jim, I have to call her."

"Here you go."

"Fuck no reception!"

"Miss Styles, are you okay," Jim asked.

She didn't speak at first, visibly shaken up and

terrified.

"He raped me! He raped me," Amanda Styles cried out.

"I'm so sorry. I'm Jim Hughes the Assistant District Attorney. You're safe now. Officer Mason is dead. The ambulance is on the way. Try and relax and everything will be okay."

The ambulances arrived. They took Amanda Styles and then put Officer Mason on a stretcher and covered him with the sheet.

"Jake, do you want to be checked out?"

"Jim, I'm fine. I just want to see Felicia."

"We'll head back to the station with Officer Bingham; you can see her for a minute than we have to ask a lot of questions."

"Yeah, fine. Can we go? There are plenty of officers to process the scene," Jake begging to leave and get back to Felicia.

JAKE

Jim and I got in the back of the cruiser and Jim shocked the shit out of me when he told me who Mason was. So, Officer Mason is David's uncle. David's father is Harold Monroe's attorney. The good thing is, it sounds like this guy was the one that was probably writing the notes.

Jim also told me that this was the cabin where David tortured Felicia. All I could picture was her disabled by his ropes and body. I feel like I'll throw up at any moment.

We got back to the station quickly as I asked them to put the sirens on and go. I had to get to Felicia. I sprinted into the Police Station. The lady up front called the Chief and told him they were back. She opened the door for me and told me where to go.

I saw her and Beth sitting at the Chief's desk. Felicia's eyes were swollen and she looked like she had seen a ghost when she looked up and saw me. She got off the chair and jumped into my arms. I couldn't hold back, I had to kiss her and hold her as tight as I could. Our tears blended on our cheeks.

"Jake, are you okay? What happened? Who took you and why," I asked with one question leading to the other.

"Angel, I'm much better now that I'm with you. The other stuff is complicated but it's over now. It's all over now. We can start our lives together and have that wedding in two weeks."

"Where's Jim," Beth asked, nervously.

"Beth, Jim will be in here in a minute. I sprinted in

here and he had to fill out some paperwork."

"Is he all right," Beth's voice was shaking.

"He's fine. You have a brave one Beth. You'd be proud of him."

Jim walked in and for the second time in a couple days, I saw Beth cry. We were both scared to death. Jake, Jim and the detectives went into the interrogation room. Many questions are unanswered. Amanda is at the hospital being treated with officers there questioning her. Officer Mason is dead but the masterminds are still alive.

Jake's statement says that Harold Monroe as well as Attorney Mason, David's father, were paying Officer Mason. David's father thought it was perfect that he was Harold's attorney and by a coincidence, the person who was behind his incarceration was the one who put his son behind bars.

Harold wanted Amanda Styles dead along with myself. He had to shut me up. I was figuring out too many things. Officer Mason told Amanda and I everything, he was planning to kill us.

After the grueling hours of questioning, it was time to go home. It was time for me to hold the love of my life. After several hours, we were able to go home.

FELICIA & JAKE

I'm not telling Jake about the texts and the letter from his father tonight. It's been a hell of a day and I think its best we just leave it for tomorrow. I need to be as close to Jake as I can be. I could've lost him today. So much of me blames myself.

"Jake, I honestly don't think I would have wanted to live if something happened to you today. So many awful things were swirling through my mind like a tornado and not one of them good. I was so scared to be without you."

"Angel, I think the scariest part for me wasn't having a gun pointed at my head but the thought of not being able to spend more time with you. I thought our time was over before it got to begin. I think my mom helped me out again today. She was watching over me."

"Jake, I believe that and I know we both have angels, real angels not the kind that is tattooed or nicknames but real angels."

"I believe that more and more. Can we not talk anymore about it though, I just want to hold you and feel you. I want to know that I'm not dreaming that you're really here."

"Want the same; I need you so much right now it is actually causing me pain."

"Felicia, I never want you to be in pain, ever."

He lifted me up off the sofa and carried me the two feet it is to the bed. Slowly, he pulled my pants off and left the laced panties on. He began massaging my feet. He kissed every toe and began to move up my calves. His calloused hands were rough and strong. He rubbed and kissed all the way to my inner thighs. He took a deep breath in and said, "Your smell is like a flower getting ready to bloom Felicia and I want to taste all of you."

My heart began to beat faster as this was still a bit uncomfortable to me. He opened my folds, licked the top of my mound, the bottom, and made out with the middle. My nub was pulsating, my hands were tearing at the sheets and my moans were getting louder. He was savoring me like his favorite yogurt. He put one finger in and was flicking it around. He added another and went harder, never letting his mouth detach from my nub. My body began to tremble like an earthquake and he sucked me all in.

"How did that feel my Angel? Did you like it?"

"It was fucking amazing! I want to do the same for you Jake."

"You do already, let me love you. I'm not ready for you to do that again to me."

JAKE

Her angel wing breasts are so fucking beautiful and perfect. I just look at them and I could explode. I take her nipples in my mouth, circling around with my tongue as I watch her thrust up against my chest. I put my hand back down to her heat and it is dripping.

"Jake, please now, can you make love to me?"

I put myself inside of her hot, wetness. She wraps her legs around me and brings me in further. I don't stop her; I need to be as deep in her as possible.

"Jake, harder, please!"

For the first time I pounded hard into her. She brought my lips to hers and tightened her grip around me. I could feel her juices surrounding me and I came with her. I lay on top of her, kissing her, holding her and I came again, this is a first. I never want to be outside of her, we're one and if I could stay like this forever, I would.

"Bright Eyes, I love you more than anything in this world. I can't wait to be your wife and have a family together.

"Angel, the love I have for you can't be put into words. It's unexplainable. It's so deep and unique and everlasting."

"I wish we could stay like this forever Jake."

"As long as I live, every day will be a day I live to make you happy and feel good. You're my home Felicia and there's no place like home as the wise Dorothy said."

We both chuckled. We lie there still naked, starving for food but not wanting to move and break the closeness between us. We fell asleep and slipped into a peaceful sleep.

FELICIA

I woke up several times throughout the night, partially because my stomach was growling and I thought I heard noises. The good thing about having a studio apartment was you didn't have to look through rooms to see if someone was there.

The place was empty but eerie feeling suddenly. I felt like someone was watching me. I rolled over to not face the window and wrapped my arm around Jake. He was sleeping and that's what was important. I spent the next hour or more watching his chest go up and down. I swear my heart was beating the same beat as his. Just watching him gave me comfort and all paranoia vanished. I fell back asleep.

I woke up to the most beautiful vision of those aqua eyes staring down at me.

"Bright Eyes, you are a vision."

"Ditto to you Angel. We're not going to work today. I called in already."

"Really? Can we stay in bed all day than?"

"Nope, we have plans to go to the church. I had your morning coffee with Beth on the phone and she's meeting us there."

"What time is it?"

"It's ten o'clock. We're meeting in an hour."

"Well, we better get going than. Can I still have a cup of coffee though?"

He smiled at me, reached over to the nightstand and handed me my favorite brew, French Vanilla. I could marry this guy. I will marry this guy.

FELICIA & BETH

We drove down to St. Vincent's church and met with the pastor. The church was exquisite. Stained glass windows, picturesque statues of the Saints making the alter what I envision heaven to look like.

The aisle was long and narrow, surrounded by pews. The view before me with my future husband standing there is actually heaven. Beth and I spoke to the pastor and set our time for the ceremony. It would be short and intimate.

"Bethy, can you believe this; in less than two weeks we'll be walking down the aisle into the arms of the loves of our lives."

"I can't wait Felicia. It's going to be the perfect day. I was thinking I don't want my parents here; I just want it to be the four of us. How about we walk each other down the aisle?"

I started to cry.

"Beth, you have to have your parents here. You're their daughter; you're only getting married once. I would love to walk down the aisle with you but your parents need to be here. I have to tell you, you are the best friend any girl could have."

"Felicia, you don't have any parents to be here and we'll have a celebration another time with my parents. I don't want anything to make you sad on our special day. Having a wedding with my best friend is all I need. "

"My mom will be with me Beth. She'll be looking

down on me and I won't be alone. I'll have all that matter with me. It's okay for them to come. I'd feel awful if they didn't."

"Well girl, the decision is already made; it will be the four of us, the pastor and the musicians and that's it.

"If you insist."

"I do. I've arranged for us to go to the Bridal Store. Jake and Jim are going to look at Tuxedos."

"Wow, I had no idea. I suppose we should do that so we are not walking down the aisle in jeans. We're running out of time, dress shopping it is. "

"Jake, you're pretty sneaky when I sleep late. You and Beth organized this whole day. Thank you," I said.

"You're welcome. Beth take good care of my angel," Jake said.

"Don't worry Jake, she's in good hands," Beth gave him a wink.

I kissed Jake on the cheek and Beth and I went in her car to the Bridal Store. Jake went to meet Jim at the Tux Shop.

JAKE & JIM

"Jake, I got some good news this morning. Harold and Cindy Monroe made a plea. They will serve twenty-five years in prison. They will have to pay each child they assaulted one million dollars. This is great news and they'll be no trial."

"This is great news. Those kids will be able to have a better life now. What about that Attorney Mason?"

"He's off the case and sitting in a jail cell probably with his son."

"What about David's parole?"

"Those records are now sealed. I can't get the information at this time. I think he would be a fucking idiot to try anything when he gets out though, his big daddy won't be there to bail him out."

"Let's hope you're right. This is good. How is Amanda Styles doing?"

"She's still in the hospital but she'll be okay physically, it's the psychological that will take time."

BETH & FELICIA

"Beth, this is the one. It's perfect. What do you think?"

"Felicia, this dress was made for you. How did you find that?"

"I told you, my mom is with me."

The dress I have chosen is pale pink chiffon. It's a straight dress with a long train flowing behind. It's sleeveless but with a sort of cowl neck, I don't know what they call it. It's simple and elegant. It's perfect for me.

Beth tried on about ten dresses and we had many laughs. She tried poufy and settled with a stunning white satin dress that was straight and then flared. It fit her style perfectly.

"Girly, we did it. We got the church and the dress. Now we just have to find you and Jake somewhere to live."

"Jeese, we haven't even had time to look. We could probably wait until after the wedding and that's fine with me. With you moving this weekend and everything else going on, I think that's best."

"Maybe you're right. Let me call Jim and see if they're finished. I'm starving; we can go out to dinner."

"We've been here that long that it's dinner time already?"

"Not quite dinner time but it's definitely cocktail time."

We left the Bridal Store after we paid for the dresses and had the measurements taken and met Jim and Jake at the Diner. Beth and I haven't been there in a while together so we thought it was a good choice.

The four of us ate big fat burgers and drank milkshakes until we were going to burst. We talked about the wedding and planned a honeymoon to Aruba. It never rains in Aruba.

The four of us will be married together and honeymoon together. This by far is the best thing that has ever happened to me. The man of my dreams and my besty!

JAKE & FELICIA

After much laughter and airy conversation, Jake and I waddled our way to door to go home. I still have to show him the letter from his father and tell him about the texts I got. No secrets.

We still can't go back to his place because they are working there on whatever damage was done. Jake is still silent about that. We got to my place, changed into comfortable clothes and sat on the sofa.

"Jake, this came for you at the office. I'm so sorry I opened it but you were missing and I thought it may give a clue."

"What's mine is yours, don't worry about it. Who's it from?"

"Open it and find out."

He opened the letter, his nostrils flared, his fists

clenched and I knew this was not going to be good. He hung his head down low and then got up and paced around the tiny room. Sweat was building on his brow and I could see the anger in his eyes.

"Jake, are you okay?"

"That son of a bitch. I'm not his son! How dare he call me that? Felicia, I will never touch you in that way. I will never hit you. You have to believe me."

"Jake, I know that. You are nothing like that man. Don't ever think you are."

"It scares me Felicia. What if I do hit you? What if he's right?"

"He's not right! He is a sick man; he's no different from Harold Monroe. You have to believe in yourself and just think of your mother. Your mother's blood is in you too and she was good from what you've told me. She would never let you mimic your father's actions."

"That fucker, he got into my head again. He's friends with David too? He's trying to make me go crazy."

"Jake, he can't make you go crazy unless you allow him to. They are only his words. It's what you do with them that matters. You can let this consume your every thought and make you think like him or you can let it go for what it is. A letter from a sick bastard that wants you to be like him but you're nothing like him.

Finding Home

Let this go and let's focus on all the good we have."

"You're right, I can't let this get to me or he wins. I'm not like him."

"There's something else. I got two texts from someone but now that we know about Officer Mason, I think it was him."

"Felicia, I'm so sorry. They have to be from him. He saw my tattoo. Okay, let's put all this negative stuff away and concentrate on you and me. I promise if I ever feel like I would hit you, I will walk away."

"Jake, you're my soul mate; I know I never have to worry about that. So put that thought to rest and let's watch a movie."

We both settled in on the sofa and watched Hangover. We needed something light and funny. Jake fell asleep on the sofa and I moved over to my bed.

He was making noises all through the night. I heard him get up and go into the bathroom. Then the retching came. He was having another nightmare. That bastard father of his brought it all back. After he came out of the bathroom and joined me in bed. I acted as if I was asleep because I didn't want him to know that I knew he had another nightmare. He laid his head on my chest and I could feel the tears wetting my t-shirt.

After a long night without sleep, I got up and made the coffee. Went out on the porch and called Beth. I told her about our night and then we talked more about the wedding and the honeymoon. She was going to arrange the trip. She's good at that. After we ended our conversation, I went back inside and took a shower. Jake was still sleeping. I didn't want to wake him after the sleepless night he had.

I called into work to let them know that Jake and I would both be late. Under the current circumstances, they understood.

I went back on the porch to relax until Jake woke up. Looking around in the common area, I noticed a small step stool in the bushes. Why would someone have a step stool outside? People are nuts. I heard a bit of mumbling from inside. Jake was stretching and waking up. I went inside, wrapped my arms around him and gave him a soft kiss on his cheek.

"Felicia, it's so late. Why didn't you wake me?"

"You looked so peaceful and I know you needed the rest. It's all set; I called work and told them we'd be late."

"You're the best Felicia; it was a rough night of sleep for me. I'll get in the shower now."

"I'll be out here, take your time. Let that water wash away the demons."

While Jake was in the shower, my cell phone rang. The call was blocked. I answered and there was no sound. I hung up figuring it was a telemarketer that takes forever for a voice to come on. For some reason, I thought of that step stool again in the yard. I find it strange that it's there.

After a while Jake came out dressed and we went off to work. He was in a daze of sorts. Still pondering over the letter he received and the kidnapping. I wish that for one day it could be a normal one.

When we got to the office, Erin had gotten everyone together to congratulate Jake and me on our engagement and to celebrate Jake being okay. Jake was quiet, more like mute. He didn't respond to any of it and he slipped into his office.

I told everyone thank you and told them that Jake was still processing what happened and he'll be fine in no time. I told them all we were having a private wedding next week. All were happy especially Erin, she's my closest friend at work.

On my desk in my office, there was an envelope with no return address. To say I was nervous about opening it was an understatement. I slowly pulled the paper back and in it was a check and a note.

Dear Miss Westfield:

Because of you, I can reclaim my life. If it weren't for you, I'd still be trapped by my cousin. I told

my wife all about it and she loves me even more now she says. I don't need money. I've had enough of Harold Monroe's money for long enough. I want no more reminders of him. Please accept my share of the settlement amount of one million dollars.

Don't try to return it. I won't accept it. You deserve it. Without you, these kids would be in hiding and afraid every day as I have been. Buy yourself a home and fill it with children.

Best Regards,

Frank Monroe

Not at all what I was expecting. Holy cow! One Million dollars. I have to go tell Jake. I ran to his office, which was only a few strides and he was sitting at his desk with his head in his hands. I put the check and the note on his desk and he looked at it. He then looked at me with shock.

"What the hell is this Felicia? Is this for real?"

"I think it is. I normally wouldn't accept anything like this but he said there was no return. This will help us buy a home and adopt, Jake."

"I can't believe this. We don't need a million dollars to find a home because we've found it already. It would help with adoption for sure though. Are you going to call him?"

"Yes, I have to thank him and make sure that this is what he wants. I'd also like to give some of it to a scholarship fund for foster kids."

"That's perfect Felicia, just as you are."

His eyes seemed to get brighter and I was seeing a glimmer of Jake. Maybe this was meant to help all of us who have been abused. I have to call Mr. Monroe. I was nervous to call him. I never had to call anyone to thank them for anything, let alone money. Nobody ever gave me anything. Having to take several deep breaths before dialing, I pressed send.

FELICIA

After calling Mr. Monroe and confirming that this was not some kind of sick joke, I sat and pondered. So much of me feels guilty for accepting this money because of how it came about. The other part of me wants to do something that will make a difference in abuse victims lives.

Beth was so excited when I told her and she said we could now buy the house next door to them that's for sale. Maybe this was fate and why Jake and I never got a chance to look for an apartment. Fate....

The next couple of days went on and there were no more surprises. Thankfully. Jake is more like himself now. We have to help Beth and Jim move today. The moving trucks have all the big stuff and we get to help unpack.

Thinking more about what Beth said about the house next to them that would be really cool. I feel joy and relief come over me that this nightmare is over. The kids are in great homes and are moving forward with adoption and Jake and I are adjusting to a bit of

normalcy even though it's only a couple days.
We're ready for the great opportunities that will take
place in our lives.

"Jake?

"Angel."

"I just want to tell you, I'm so happy with you. I can't
wait to be your wife. I want to spend every day
showing you how much I love you. Together we can
get through anything. We've done it thus far and it
hasn't been an easy ride."

"Felicia, I never thought I could be happy in my life.
You bring me sunshine even through the clouds. I will
dedicate my life to make you happy and keep you safe.
I love you today, tomorrow and always."

He stepped closer to me, backed me up against the
wall and with a hand on each side of my face, he
brought his lips to mine. This kiss had meaning; it was
the seal to our love and devotion to each other. I
couldn't stop at the kiss; I wanted this man and had to
have him. Our tongues were dancing, our bodies
rhythmically thrusting together to become one. The
passion was raw and deep as he had me against the
wall. Nobody else existed in this world but the two of
us making hard love. We both came unglued together
and slid down to the floor in pleasure.

"Felicia, you make my insides crazy. Holy Shit, I may
need a minute to recover."

I laughed at him and I was strangely ready for more.

"I wish I could say what you do to me, but it's very Dirty Bright Eyes."

"Please whisper it to me later. Right now we have to pick up your revolver,.38 Special then go to Beth and Jim's to slave away the day."

"Jake, I don't need the gun anymore. Do we have to get it?"

"No questions please. You'll like having it when you get it. You have to be able to protect yourself if I'm not with you. Sorry Angel, you can't win this one."

I never thought I would ever carry a gun. I know he's right to a point but I still think he's overreacting. Off we went to the Gun and Tackle Store. Maybe if I gave this weapon a name it wouldn't scare me so much. Janie, that's what I'll name it. Janie was the name of my doll when I was little and she always made me feel safe at night.

After picking up the gun, I wanted to shoot a little to practice. We went to the range and I was a really good shot. Jake showed me all the ins and outs of it and I felt more at ease with it. Janie will come everywhere with me. Now Beth and I will both be badass. We headed over to Beth and Jim's to help them unpack.

The movers are carrying furniture and the sweat is

beading off them. Jim and Beth are inside unpacking the bedroom things. I told her I wasn't unpacking her sexy lingerie and toys. Jake and I started in the kitchen and unpacked dishes and glasses. We were having fun joking around.

Beth and Jim were having their own fun teasing each other with their bedroom accessories. After hours of sweating and unpacking, we took a break with Jim and Beth and had pizza.

"Felicia, I forgot to tell you, I set up an appointment for you and Jake to look at the house next door," Beth said.

"Are you my personal secretary now Beth? When is it," I asked chuckling.

"Oh Shit, the realtor will be here in a half an hour. We better finish eating fast," Beth blurted.

"Jake, are you okay with that," I asked.

"Like I said before, home is where you are. What the hell, let's take a look," Jake said grabbing my hand.

We chatted for a few more minutes and just seeing how excited Beth and Jim were about their new home, I wanted the same. The realtor knocked on Beth's door and the four of us went next door to take a look.

We walked in to an open foyer with a staircase in front of us. The staircase was open and you could see upstairs from below and vise versa. We walked into the kitchen, it was tiled floors, granite counters, stainless steel appliances, a hood over the stove and a double wall oven. It is stunning. The family room's cathedral ceilings and floor to ceiling fireplace made me want this house.

"Jake, do you like it?"

"I'll let you know. I have to see the bedroom first. That's where I plan to spend the best part of my day with you."

"One track mind Jake. Let's go take a look upstairs then."

There were four bedrooms upstairs and two full bathrooms. This house is spectacular.

"Let's do it Felicia. The master bedroom has a Jacuzzi and enough room for a king sized bed for when all the kids come and sleep with us when there's a thunder storm."

Tears began to fall and I hugged him so tight. This is the perfect house for us. The big back yard already had a swing set and a sandbox. I never could afford anything half as nice as this if it wasn't for that check.

We put our offer in and the realtor called the bank, as it was bank owned. We went back to Beth and Jim's and waited for the call.

Finding Home

Jim and Jake went out on the screened in porch and had a beer. Beth and I went upstairs to the bedroom and chatted. We were both so happy. I'm hoping we really get the house next door. Beth and I are lying on her bed and doing our daydream thing when the phone rang. I jumped up and answered.

"Felicia Westfield speaking."

"Sorry, wrong number."

I know that voice. Whose voice was it? I can't place it. The phone rang again.

"Hello?"

"Felicia, it's Robin, the bank accepted your offer. Congratulations."

"Thank you so much. When can we move in?"

"The bank likes to move on these pretty quick. How does two weeks sound to you?"

"I'll be on my honeymoon; can we make it that Monday after?"

"I'm sure that will be fine. I have all your paper work and I'll set up the inspection and such. Congratulations it's a beautiful home."

"Thank you Robin."

I hung up the phone and Beth and I jumped around and danced. We ran down the stairs to tell Jim and Jake we're going to be neighbors. We all celebrated with a beer. Jake also wanted to celebrate the fact that I got the gun.

"Beth, did Felicia tell you she's packing now," Jake said with a winning smile.

"NO! You did it girl? We are two badass chicks. Don't misfire whatever you do."

"I can't believe I forgot to tell you. We just got it before coming here. I named it Janie so it didn't seem as scary to me. I better not misfire. Now you got me paranoid about that."

Such a surreal moment in realizing how my life has changed so much since meeting Jake. My heart is full and finally living the dream. Jake and I left to give Jim and Beth some time alone in their new home. We talked about adopting and even fostering kids to fill the bedrooms in the new house.

"Jake, I want to fill the house with kids. Just like Frank Monroe said. I want to share our love with a house full of kids."

"Let's do it than. Right after the wedding we'll move in and fill it up with kids. I've never loved you more than I do this moment. You're going to be the best mommy."

"And you will be the best daddy."

FELICIA

This weekend flew by and the week ahead will go just as fast. We have to pack up two apartments before the wedding so we'll be ready right when we get back from Aruba. We have to fill out all the paper work to become foster parents, which should be a breeze. Beth and I have to go to our fitting for our dresses and the men have to go for their tuxedos.

Jake and I are wishing we took this week off too; we hadn't planned to buy a house though so there wasn't enough notice. We packed Jake's apartment yesterday. It was freshly painted, so I'm not sure what kind of damage the intruder did. He doesn't have nearly as much as I do but that doesn't say much.

Jake turned in his keys and said good-bye to his apartment. We went back to my place to face another set of boxes. We were too tired to do anymore today so we ordered Chinese takeout. We took our food and sat on the porch to eat. Something caught my eye. The step stool was under my window now. Is someone watching us? I didn't say a word in hopes that Jake didn't see it. From where he was sitting, he shouldn't. I didn't want him to start freaking out.

After dinner we went and showered together. A shower is never the same to me anymore. I am now confident in my own skin, inked and all. I thrive on his touch and he mine. After our hot shower, we both crawled into bed with satisfied hungers. Jake draped his arm over me as he always does and I fell sleep with my head on his Maple Leaf.

"Jake, wake up. Did you see that?"

"What? What is it? Are you okay?"

"I'm fine; there was just a flash of light through the window."

Jake got up out of bed with his boxers on and went out on the porch. He didn't see anyone but he saw the tipped over step stool. He came back in and called the police to have them check the area.

"Did you see anything Jake?"

JAKE

"No, it could have been lightening but the police will check the area just in case. Go back to sleep Angel, everything is fine."

Finding Home

Fuck! Someone was obviously out there. I'm so glad she has that gun. She wasn't falling back asleep too fast and I knew this night was not going to be filled with sleep for me. I rubbed her temples and her hair to help her fall back asleep and she gave in and did.

In the morning I called the Police Station to see if there was anything out of the ordinary and they informed me that there had been a few break ins at the apartment complex but they thought it was just teenagers looking for booze money. They would have the place put on their hot sheet.

I think I feel a bit of relief knowing that this isn't a random thing. We'll just keep our eyes and ears open. We'll be out of here in less than a week anyway.

"Felicia, rise and shine Angel. Time to go to work. Your coffee is ready and the shower is running for you."

"Will you be joining me this morning Jake?"

Thankful that she wasn't bringing up last night, I don't want this to ruin the week for her.

"I've already showered; I'm going to wait on the porch for you."

"Bummer."

I went on the porch to drink my coffee and looked over to where the tipped over step stool was and it was gone. I then went inside and checked all the locks on the windows again. All locked. It probably just was some kids.

We got to the office and things were much better. No real investigations going on right now and that's great. Felicia and I filled out the paper work to become foster parents while we were at work. Everything was going good and quiet.

Felicia was getting over the moon excited about the wedding and her fitting. Erin was going to have a small surprise shower for her tomorrow. It's going to happen; she'll be my wife before this time next week. I can't wait.

"Hello Bright Eyes. Are you busy?"

"Never too busy for you. Not busy at all actually and I kind of like it. What can I do for you Angel?"

I sat on his lap, ran my fingers through his hair and kissed him with everything I had.

"That's what I wanted Jake. I love you."

"You can do that anytime but I suggest not here because now I can't leave my office for a bit."

"No apologies. I'm going to finish up and go meet Beth at the Dress Shop."

"You seem a little excited. You are going to be the

most beautiful bride there ever was Felicia."

"I'm so excited Jake. I hope you like my dress."

"I'll love you in it and out of it."

"Okay, it's getting too hot in here, I have to finish up quick."

Is it possible to be the happiest woman that has ever lived? Nothing could ruin this for us. I'm soon to be Mrs. Felicia Brown; I love the ring to that.

My phone rang and it was a blocked number.

"Hello, Felicia Westfield."

"Sorry wrong number."

"It's okay have a great day."

The line went dead. Lots of wrong numbers but that voice was the same. I can't put my finger on it. I hate that. I can't let it get to me.

FELICIA & BETH

I left the office to go meet Beth at the Bridal Shop. This is it; we're both going to be brides within hours, not weeks or months... hours.

Beth came out of her dressing room with her gown and veil on. She is simply stunning. She turned to the mirror in front of her and cried. This in turn made me cry. She and I have been through everything together and now it's our time to shine.

"Bethy, you are so beautiful. Jim will melt like a puddle when you walk down that aisle."

"I love it and I especially love sharing this with you Felicia. It's your turn girl; go get your dress on."

"Okay, it better fit. There's no time to spare."

I can't help but feel a twinge of guilt that her mom won't be there to see her in her happiest moment. Beth is a stubborn and selfless woman; she's putting me in front of her and I love her.

I slipped into the dress and the tailor zipped it in the back. It fit like a glove. I walked out to see Beth and she didn't speak.

"Beth, what is it? Is it bad?"

"I knew you were always beautiful Felicia, but right now, there are no words to describe how you look. The glow on your face, the shimmering from your eyes makes that pink snap back at you and reflect whole happiness and beauty. I've been waiting a long time to see you this happy. I love you girl."

We're both crying happy tears now. Beth and I sharing this once in a lifetime moment together is priceless. We had the woman take pictures of us in our gowns.

We sauntered all over the shop and practiced how we would walk down the aisle. This was so Beth's style.

With the dress in one hand and Beth's in my other, this was a happy moment. Beth will keep my dress at her house and we'll get ready there. The guys should be done with their tuxedo fitting by now.

Beth and I went our separate ways and all of a sudden, I got another one of those goddamn bad feelings in my gut. It has to be just anxiety. Nothing will ruin my mood. I turned up the music and sang until I got to my place. Trying hard to push the feeling in my gut away.

JAKE & FELICIA

Jake was surrounded by boxes when I got home. He's sitting on the floor looking at a photo of my mother and me when I was five years old. He didn't even look up when I walked in.

"Hey Bright Eyes. I see you found my pictures."

"Felicia, you look exactly like your mother. She has the same kind eyes as you and everything; it's as if you are twins."

"I haven't looked at this picture in years. It hurts too much at times. She's about my age now in this picture. She's much more beautiful than I'll ever be, she's an angel."

I couldn't help but let the tears flow. I could feel my mother's arms around me, protecting me and loving me.

"Felicia, you are every bit as beautiful as she was. She would be so proud of you if she were here."

"She is here. I feel her. She loves you too Jake."

"Well, I love her too because she brought you to me. How did the fitting go?"

"It was awesome; Beth and I had the best time. The dress is ready and so am I. How about your tux?"

"All set here too. Everything's working out great Felicia. Before we know it, we'll be in our home tucking kids in to bed and then making love in ours."

"That sounds like heaven right there. We really are going to live happily ever after. Our scars are fading Jake with every passing day."

"It's all because of you Angel."

"It's all because of Fate!"

Erin put on a small bridal shower for me at the office. It was co-ed. They gave me some nice things and some not so nice things if you know what I mean. They even had a few gifts for the groom. It was wonderful and I'm feeling very blessed.

Jake and I have been approved for foster parents and we're both excited. I'm hoping to get a baby, as is he. Today is getting all the details in order for the big day. I'll be sleeping away from Jake tonight since the first day we met. Not completely away, we're both staying at Beth and Jim's tonight but Beth and I are having a bachelorette party sleep over. The men will be sleeping downstairs having their own manly thing.

Jim brought us food and beverage and we had all we needed to seclude ourselves from our men. Beth and I did our nails, than took another sip of wine. We did a trial run with our hair and makeup. It was any girl's dream.

We were tempted to put our gowns on but we decided it was bad luck. We didn't want anything to get in the way of our weddings. After we were finished with the beauty aspect of our girl's night we continued down memory lane.

We laughed until god knows what time and finally fell asleep. The guys never came up once; I think if they had, Beth would have shot them. You do not screw with Beth! The guys watched sports and drank lots of beer until they passed out.

FELICIA & BETH

Beth and I woke up to the pleasing aroma of coffee and muffins. The wedding is at noon. Jim and Jake left before we got up and went to pack up the rest of my apartment. They'll get ready there. The next time we see them, they will be standing on the alter waiting for Beth and I.

"Felicia, we cannot be late today. I promised Jim and Jake that I would make sure we were not late. One day girly, that's all I ask."

"Bethy, this is one day I won't be late for! Don't you worry, I'll be ready but we should start soon. The limo is coming at 11:15."

Beth and I showered, did each other's hair and makeup and it was time to put the dresses on. We both stood in front of her full-length mirror to make sure we looked perfect for our men.

"Girl, we are two fucking badass hot girls. Are you ready? The limo should be here any minute."

"I'm ready Beth. I've never been more ready for anything in my life. The limo driver said he would call when he pulled up front. Speak of the devil, this must be him."

"Hello?"

"I'm out front; the door is open for you."

"Thank you."

That voice. It's the same voice with the wrong number. I knew I knew that voice. He must have had my number programmed into his phone wrong.

Beth and I walked outside to the limo and the new neighbors were all gawking to see who was getting in the limo. Beth got in the limo first and I followed.

The limo wasn't a huge limo, it only seated six. The driver pulled away from the curb after putting up the glass between the front and the back. When the glass closed, there was a letter taped to it. It read,

"Congratulations! Open Now!"

"Oh God Felicia, I'm sure Jake left you a long love letter. Open it; I can't wait to see what he wrote. He's so cheesy sometimes."

I opened the envelope and pulled out a piece of paper. It wasn't a note. It was a picture. I unfolded it. I stared at it. Not able to move. Beth grabbed it from me and didn't say a word either.

The limo was dangerously quiet. My body and mind at this time doesn't know what to do. The picture is of me tied up with blood all over me. David took this picture. The other picture was of Jake and me making love. Then I found a note inside that said:

I told you I'd see you soon. This is the end for you Felicia. You will never be Mrs. Felicia Brown.

HAHAHAHA

David

Beth and I are planning in our silence. We both tried our doors but they were locked and the controls were up front. The glass partition came down and he spoke. That voice was David's all along.

DAVID, FELICIA & BETH

David lowered the glass so we could hear him.

"Didn't I tell you Felicia that you were mine," David said with a devious voice.

Silence.

"Answer me fucking Angel," David screamed.

"Don't call me that David. You'll never get away with this," I said with a shaky voice.

"Don't underestimate me Angel," David said.

Beth tried to keep quiet. I could see her fists clenching and I knew the time was here that she was going to say something.

"Listen you cock sucker, let her out of this limo. You can duel it out with me instead," Beth said adamantly.

"Oh Beth, you haven't changed. Always to the little fucking Felicia's rescue. Sorry, she's all mine now. I'm never letting her go alive," David replied.

"David, you are such a weak, twisted daddy's boy that thinks he can do anything without accountability. I've got news for you, you fucking monster! Your daddy can't get you out of this one," Beth says without any fear.

Now that Beth and David are having words, I am getting increasingly anxious. She is firing him up even more.

"David, where are we going," I asked.

"To our place. Only this time I'm going to make damn sure nobody will ever have you again. You seem to really like the fucking thing huh Felicia," David said like poison.

"David, I'm not yours and yes I do love to make love to Jake. He makes my body shake when he makes me cum. It's something you never did to me. Jake loves my body and he has felt and tasted every part of it," I said trying to get to him.

"You fucking whore, Felicia. You will never fuck him again! It's over. You and this Jake pansy will never see each other again and I will have the last fuck," David screamed definitively.

"David, you can kill me but at least I know that I died loved and sexually satisfied which is more than I can say for you," I shouted to him.

JIM & JAKE

Meanwhile back at the church, Jim and Jake are looking at their watches.

"Jim, I thought you said Beth was going to make Felicia on time."

"I did and she promised she would be here ten minutes early."

"I have a bad feeling something isn't right. Do you know what limo company they were using again?"

"Felicia arranged it but I think I remember Beth telling

me it was Sunshine Limo Services."

"I'm calling them to see if the Limo left on time. Maybe they got caught in traffic or there was an accident."

"Jim, the limo service said the driver left an hour and half ago. They said that the girls were picked up as they have to push a button in the limo to let them know they arrived."

"Give me your phone Jake, I'm calling back. I want the license plate number."

Dialing the phone...

"This is Assistant District Attorney Jim Hughes; my fiancée is in a limo that has not arrived at the church yet. I want the license plate number. Thank you."

Jim called the police and told them to put an all out bulletin on a white limo, license plate number- **SNSHN5**.

"Jim, do you have your phone on you? If Felicia has her phone with her, we can track it. I don't have a Smartphone."

"Yeah, I have it in the back room."

Jim handed me the phone and I was able to quickly download the app on his phone and look up Felicia's phone. My legs went numb.

"Fuck Jim, they're heading for that cabin. We got to get there before it's too late."

"Let's go! I'll drive and you keep watching where they're at. Give me your phone so I can call for back up."

"It's David. It has to be."

"Jake, I'm sorry but I think you're right."

DAVID, FELICIA & BETH

In the limo, the girls are keeping it together very well. Beth is motioning with her eyes to Felicia and they are still in planning mode.

"Beth, it's been a long time since I had any pussy. I've always wanted to fuck you and it sure looks like it's my lucky day."

"Shut the fuck up David. There's no way you are getting anywhere near my golden mound."

"I think you're wrong. Ask Felicia. When I want something I get it."

"It looks like it David. You've been in prison getting fucked up the ass I'm sure while Felicia found love. That to me sounds like you are a loser all the way around."

David is getting more pissed each time there is conversation. His eyes in the rear view mirror are of fire. Beth is moving in her seat, waiting for the Limo to stop. My heart is in my throat.

JIM & JAKE

"Jim, step on it! They're pulling down that dirt road. He's going to kill them."

"Jake, I'm going ninety, we'll get there. I promise you. If not, I'll never forgive myself."

DAVID

The limo stops. David turns around for the first time. Up until this point I could only see his eyes in the rearview mirror. Seeing his face again makes me sick to my stomach.

"Oh Felicia, you sure do make a beautiful bride. I'm so happy that I got out in time to see you."

"Fuck off David," I exclaimed.

"Oooh, did Beth teach you how to talk like that?"

"Yeah she did along with other things."

"Which do you prefer? Do you want me to fuck you ladies in here or inside your favorite cabin Felicia?"

"You aren't fucking either of us David," Beth yelled out.

He got out of the front seat, opened my door first, pulled me by my hair and held me tight. He fucking bit my ear. He dragged me over to Beth's door and pulled her out with his other hand. He must have been working out in prison because he never had these muscles before.

He brought us both into the cabin. Shivers covered my entire body seeing it again. He threw both of us on the bed and was about to tie us up when Beth lifted her hand. I've never been less afraid of a gun before.

"Look at the two of you; on the happiest day of your lives and you're here with me. It's so kind of you both to have dressed up for me. I'm going to make up for lost time and fuck you both! Then I'm going to end you."

David got my left hand tied to the headboard. Meanwhile, Beth had signaled to me that she had a gun under her gown. A bit of relief enveloped me. He grabbed Beth's arm and began to tie a knot around her wrist.

With my right hand, I carefully slid my hand under Beth's dress and felt the small Glock 26 9mm being held by her garter belt. I carefully took the gun from under her gown with my right hand that he was going to tie together with Beth's. I held it up to David and he was in shock. I never thought I could pull the trigger of a gun at someone but the adrenaline and the fear and the need for survival kicked in.

"You fucking sick bastard, look at me. Look into my eyes. You will never fuck me again; you will never have power over me again. You are a dead man and there's nothing that will give me more pleasure. You think you have the power? David, I have all the power now and pulling this trigger will give me more pleasure than you will ever know." I cowered in his face.

"You don't have the guts to pull the trigger Angel," David replied with a bit of doubt.

"Just look at me David; this is the last vision you will ever see," I said with pleasure.

David looked me right in the eye and I shot him, dead center. He tumbled on top of us on the bed. Blood spatter staining our dresses. We heard car doors slamming and saw blue lights.

Jim and Jake ran through the door without warning. Not having a clue if they would be shot. They saw Beth and me lying underneath David's still body, covered in blood but they saw us breathing. Both big men began to cry to match Beth and me.

The police came in along with the EMT and removed David's body from atop of us. They put David's body on a stretcher and covered it with a white sheet. Neither Beth nor I could move. We were in shock.

Jake came over to me and I couldn't even speak. Jim on the other side went to Beth. She cried out all the tears she has held in for all her years.

"Jim, I have never been more scared in all of my life. He was going to rape us and kill us. I had to do it," Beth cried out.

"Baby, it's okay. It's over now, he got what he had coming to him. He deserved it and it was self-defense. The important thing is that you two are okay. I love you so much Beth," Jim said while holding Beth tight.

"Oh Jim, I love you too. I'm so sorry about the wedding. Is it too late," Beth asked.

"I think we'll make other plans. Jake, is she okay," Jim asked concerned for Felicia.

"She's just staring at me Jim. We need to get her to the hospital. We need to call another ambulance and I won't have her riding with that bastard's dead body."

The ambulance came and transported Beth and Felicia to the hospital. Beth appeared to be in a lot better mental state than Felicia was. Chief Marrin came down to the do the questioning in the hospital room.

They found two knives on David and a .38 that was laying on the bed. It's being deemed self-defense. Beth was free to go but she wouldn't leave her best friend's side. The doctor's gave Felicia a sedative in hopes that she will relax enough to speak.

She fell asleep while Jake, Beth and Jim stayed by her side. After a few hours, she woke up and had no idea where she was but she spoke.

"Jake, I pulled the trigger. I killed him," I sobbed.

Jake looked quizzically at Beth and Jim.

"It's okay Angel. You did the right thing and you were protecting yourself," Jake said.

Beth came closer to me and looked at me.

"Felicia, I shot him girl. You know I did," Beth said, while staring into my eyes to have me understand she was taking the blame.

"Beth, you don't need to cover for me. I'm okay with it. I want to own the fact that I stopped him from hurting others and potentially us. You're the best friend anyone could ever have and I thank you for having your piece with you, but I shot him."

"Okay girl," Beth agreed.

Jim and Jake looked at Beth and she shook her head at them.

"Jake, did we get married?"

"No Angel, we didn't but we can right now if you

want."

She looked around the room with her glazed over eyes.

"Beth, will you be my maid of honor?"

She laughed aloud and said, "As long as you don't mind I have the same Johnny on as you."

"That's perfect Beth."

Jim was a justice of the peace so he married us in the hospital room.

"I now pronounce you husband and wife. You may kiss the bride," Jim, the ADA and JP said.

Jake kissed me long and soft. I'm now Mrs. Jake Brown. Looks like I won in the end David.

EPILOGUE

I was released from the hospital the following day as Mrs. Felicia Brown. The honeymoon was postponed to a later date. Beth and Jim got married in their back yard with me as the maid of honor, Jake as the best man, her mother as a bridesmaid and her father as a groomsman.

Jake and I moved in to our new house and our first houseguests besides Mr. and Mrs. James Hughes were Kayla, Joey and Adam. We both wished that we could adopt them but they were happy with the Harpers and it was where they should stay.

After a month in our home, we became foster parents to our first child. Olivia, a two-month-old baby left for dead on a church doorstep. She was the most beautiful thing I had ever seen. Jake fell in love for the second time in his life.

I quit my job at Social Services and opened up a center for abused children. Jake went and worked at the District Attorney's office. When Olivia was six months old Jake and I adopted her. She's now Olivia Brown.

I did end up looking for my father. He had a family and he was clean and sober. I can't say that it didn't hurt that he never cared to contact me but forgiveness had to be given. There's been too much hurt and pain. The past had to be rectified and the scars are faded now. Although he doesn't feel like my dad, I have made amends.

Jake and I started to visit our mother's graves every Sunday. It was nice to sit and tell them how everything is. We felt closer to them, almost as if they were still here.

Kayla, Joey, Adam and Daniel are all happy and healthy in their adoptive homes. They come to our home often to play with baby Olivia. Their scars have started to heal and Daniel even has a girlfriend now.

Mr. and Mrs. Monroe were getting pay back in prison. They were getting what they deserve. Even criminals don't like pedophiles. Mrs. Monroe shares a cell with a Big Bertha, its comical at the very least.

Jake's father was found dead in his cell by suicide. Jake had no sadness and hoped that his visit did get to him. After his death, Jake finally had closure on his past.

Frank Monroe moved to Florida with his family to start his life over without constant reminders of his past. He left the newspaper business and went on to write self- help books. He gave the newspaper to his dear friend, Amanda Styles.

David's father was disbarred and was sentenced to five years in jail. He lost his home and his wife.

Captain Murphy served six months in prison and was put on parole for five years. He had to attend gamblers anonymous and do three hundred hours of community service.

This was a wild ride. So much sadness and pain. Happiness and love was found and in the end, we all found HOME!

THE END

A Note from the Author

Thank you for taking the time and reading Finding Home. I apologize if there is any confusion with the dialogue. I wanted it all to flow as a real conversation. I tried to label, so I hope you weren't confused!

I understand that some parts of this book may have troubled some. It did me as well but I had to write it. As horrific, unfair and oh so damaging to one's self esteem and whole mental state, my message is clear. If you or someone you know have been abused, either a child or an adult, there is hope to find your home.

The scars never do go away but a new hope can be given. Always fight for justice and never be ashamed. Never be afraid to tell someone. You have a voice that deserves to be heard.

Jake and Felicia's love was instant and I know that this is fiction, but I believe in their case, they were meant to be together and the time and the connection they shared were aligned.

I hope you enjoyed this book. I enjoyed writing it. Many times through the tears.

Please take a moment and write a review on **www.amazon.com** I will not be offended if it is a bad review, it will make me strive to be better!

Thank you for reading,   Abbey K Davies.

ABOUT THE AUTHOR

Abbey K Davies is her penname. She started writing fiction in 2012 and has found a great passion for it.

Being fiction for her doesn't mean there cannot be a lesson in each book she writes. She strives to make a print on your heart with her writing.

She is married with two kids. She is a business owner and life coach as well. She lives in New Hampshire.

Her other books are:

What Lies Under the Weeping Willow- PASSION

What Lies Under the Weeping Willow- REVENGE

The Fire Inside

They can all be found at: **www.amazon.com** and **www.bn.com**
https://www.facebook.com/abbeyk.davies

If you can send a review to **www.amazon.com** it would greatly be appreciated.

Thank you, Abbey

Finding Home

Abbey K Davies